I0586331

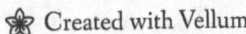

Gate Sinister

A Tale of Treacherous Fairies, Governessing in Gothic Manors, Vile Enchantments, Phantasmagoric Philtres & Extraordinary Devices, the Entirely Lost & Not-Quite-Found Forest of Arden, Magical Artifice & the Science of Miracles in 19th Century Britannia.

Tansy Rayner Roberts

Contents

CHANCERY SISTERS MAKE THEIR MATCHES

Love is in the air in London this season, and thanks to the continuing fashion for love philtres, it does not have to be left to happenstance! Don't forget to keep your vial of antidote close by, in case the wrong suitor tries to take advantage. Let's hope those rumours about a shortage of pure Love-Me-Not are without foundation — we don't want to return to the dark days of the Prince Regent's reign, when love philtres had no cure.

Once again, our city fills with hopeful young ladies and dashing young gentlemen, armed with dowries and titles to exchange in the thrilling sport we like to call The Marriage Market. The talk of the town this year is the beautiful and wealthy Chancery sisters. Their father set out to catch the very best husbands for his gold-plated darlings — and didn't he do well?

This periodical already reported on the wedding of Miss Elspeth Chancery to the invalid Lord Mortmain of Bath earlier this month. Someone's looking to be a merry widow sooner rather than later. Was she after his title or his extensive magical library?

Now the new Lady Mortmain's sister has landed a lord of her own. Miss Carolinge Chancery is engaged to be married to the impoverished but highly eligible Lord Salisbury Gloucester, heir to the Earl of Shuttlesworth, not to mention the famous Love-Me-Not fortune.

No comment yet on whether Miss Carolinge will take a philtre on her wedding day, to ensure her Happy Ever After.

Watch this space!

— A London Gossip, *The Spark and Philtre Gazette*, 1862

Chapter 1

In Which Miss Wednesday is Snubbed By a House

Kent, Britannia, 1878

The house closed around Flavia as she stepped across the threshold. The wallpaper in this hallway was dark and imposing, with spiral patterns you couldn't stare at too closely without getting a headache. Every piece of furniture was a perfectly preserved piece of ancient history, weighed down by years of buffing and polishing.

Gloucester Worth. Even the name of the place sounded heavy, and ominous. It told you something about the Gloucester family, that they should name their country seat in such a ponderous manner.

No one ever named a house Gloucester Delight, or Gloucester Whimsy. Flavia was sure she would not enjoy a house called Whimsy, as she was in the process of rebelling against a highly whimsical childhood, but she was certain she could never live up to Worth.

Graves the butler, walking ahead of her with measured steps, was himself an antique; an elderly gentleman in a suit as crisp as folded paper. His expression was neutral, leaving Flavia in no doubt that this was the only time she would ever be allowed through the front door.

As this paragon of a butler led the way up a whirl of a staircase, everything about the house said: *we are better than you.*

Flavia pretended not to notice. This was a job interview and not a contest of wills. At least, she hoped so.

Mrs Holloway the housekeeper met them at the top of the stairs, a matronly figure in a flawless black dress. She had already interviewed Flavia in London, winnowing down a list of several young and suitable 'gels' to find the right candidate for this position.

"Lady Carolinge prefers demure females who know their place," Mrs Holloway said as she swept along the landing. "See you don't embarrass me." She opened a door and thrust Flavia inside, closing it behind her with a click. Between one breath and another, Flavia stepped from a dark, disapproving monolith of a house into a bright and beautiful drawing room that held no ill will against her at all.

It was a shock. The drawing room was all lemons

and peaches, bathed in the light that poured through the window.

The house might disapprove of Flavia, but this room had taken a liking to her. That was a good start.

Her potential employer sat at a cream-coloured tea table. The Honourable Lady Carolinge Gloucester, daughter-in-law to the Earl of Shuttlesworth, was impossibly elegant. She was pale yellow, from the sheen of her fashionable hair arrangement to the sweep of her morning gown and (as no amount of powder could disguise) her unfortunately sallow complexion.

Following the theme of yellow, yellow, yellow, the Hon. Lady Carolinge pursed her lips as if she had been sucking lemons. "Wednesday," she said. "What sort of name is that?"

Mine, thought Flavia. *And it sounds more human than the one I was born with.* "My family are from Somerset," she said aloud, widening her eyes with pretend honesty.

A look of quiet horror passed over Lady Carolinge's face. "At least you've done something about your accent," she approved.

"I do my best," replied Flavia, fighting the urge to start speaking like a yokel.

"Your references are excellent, and Mrs Holloway thinks you eminently suitable for this position." Lady Carolinge sounded unconvinced.

"I enjoyed my last position at Dorchester Grove very much," Flavia said politely.

Lady Carolinge leaped upon this opportunity to criticise. "Then why did you leave?"

Goodness, did the woman even want to hire a governess? Anyone would think she felt threatened by Flavia's plain day dress, her thick-waisted figure and not-quite-polished vowels. "The children grew up," she said, which was the honest truth.

"You're very young."

This was like walking on porcelain. Expensive, angry porcelain that wanted to catch you out, and yank your hair. "I'm one and twenty. I went to the Earnsley family straight out of training, three years ago, when their old governess retired due to ill health. Kitty and Sarah were the only daughters not yet out. Now they have gone to be finished in Switzerland."

Finished. As if turning fifteen meant that frocks and table manners were suddenly more important than books. Mind you, this was true for Kitty and Sarah Earnsley of Dorchester Grove. The only point of books, as far as they and their mother were concerned, was to have something to balance on one's head during deportment exercises. Still, they had been kind, and grateful for Flavia's unique abilities beyond the schoolroom.

The swarm of pixies that infested their rose garden would not make a reappearance any time soon, and Sarah Earnsley would be able to marry without explaining to a future husband why she set fire to her lace handkerchief every time she sneezed.

"My children are extremely delicate," said Lady Carolinge, watching Flavia like a hawk.

Delicate. That was one of those words, like bright and sensitive and special, which had a very specific definition in polite society. A definition you would never find in the dictionary.

"I can handle that," said Flavia. "Looking after delicate children with unique sensibilities is a specialty of mine." She could be as mealy-mouthed as the rest of them.

"Indeed." The interview was at an end. Lady Carolinge stood up so quickly that she was almost impolite. "Your salary is thirty pounds a year, Miss Wednesday, from which you are expected to purchase all of your clothes. You must present yourself with decorum and the appearance of a respectable young lady at all times, especially when escorting the children in public. You will have a room to yourself in the attic, and a half day off every other Wednesday."

Flavia's eyebrow quirked. She couldn't help it.

Lady Carolinge blinked, oddly unsettled. "Every other Thursday," she decided instead. "Do you have any questions?"

"What are the children's names, please?" Flavia asked.

"Petronella and Dashmond."

Oh, she must not laugh. Who was she to mock, in any case, carrying around a name like Flavia in a sea of Susans, Bettys and Isoldas?

"I shall be glad to join your household," Flavia said meekly.

"Indeed," said the Honourable Lady Carolinge with a sniff. "I should think so."

The door was flung open in a hurry. The Honourable Lord Salisbury Gloucester, heir to the Earl of Shuttlesworth and master of the house, strode in. A bluff, rotund fellow, he was altogether more amiable than his wife. Lady Carolinge's face changed instantly upon his appearance as if he had brought even more sunshine into the room with him. "My dear," she cooed, sweet lemon pie instead of sour fruit. "This is our new governess. She came highly recommended."

"Capital," said Lord Salisbury with a wave of his hand – a useful gesture for him to employ when meeting someone who was not quite a servant, but still not worth bothering about. "Glad to know you, Miss... The pups are a bit of a handful, but I'm sure they'll knuckle down to work with a strong hand at the helm, what!"

The Honourable Carolinge simpered. "My husband has everyone's measure, Miss Wednesday," she said with a doting smile.

"Wednesday, eh?" bellowed Lord Salisbury. "Not related to that lady author with the whimsical elves and the toadstools and the whatnot, are you? Loved those books when I was a lad."

Lady Carolinge froze as if in horror, then smiled at

her husband as if he had said something wonderfully clever. "No, dearest, she is of the Somerset Wednesdays."

"That's all right then," said Lord Salisbury, patting his wife as if she was a dog. "Lady of the house doesn't approve of toadstool stories," he said with a wink.

Flavia knew straight away that she preferred the snappish shrew from her interview over this soft, simpering foot-cushion that Lady Carolinge became in her husband's presence. She was never going to like Lord Salisbury no matter how generously he treated his staff.

This was clearly a love philtre marriage. An unequal one, in which the wife had taken the dose, and the husband had not.

It was enough to make you sick to your stomach.

Still, their disturbing marital choices made no difference to her. Flavia was here for the children.

∽

A room to herself was an unexpected bonus. Flavia was shown to a clean but drab attic, divided into small rooms for the female servants. Her space had a steep, sloping ceiling, a wobbly wall and a corner of a window, which disappeared into the plastered partition.

She was lucky not to have to share with the maids as she had at her previous situation. The bed squeaked like it was designed that way (more of a protection than an annoyance, for a young woman in service). There was a lopsided and cheaply produced portrait of Her Majesty, Queen Isolda, Empress of Britannia and India, hanging above the metal frame of the bed.

Several of the Queen's pretty daughters were arrayed beside her, all painted with pale skin and carefully arranged dark curls above the old-fashioned Elizabethan neck-ruffs that had been a court fashion a few years ago. An old portrait, then, from before the doomed marriages took their toll on the Royal Family's public image. There were fewer daughters in the more recently-distributed public portraits, many of them in mourning black like their mother, all of them looking thoroughly disgruntled.

Only when she sat at the wobbly dressing table, with small basin and mirror, did Flavia begin to shake. She had been holding herself in for so long, maintaining control. As she gave way to the exhaustion, a leaf-green colour glazed across her skin, up her arms from elbows to fingertips. Her neatly bundled yellow hair flooded green as well, and she allowed it to be free for the moment.

She was here, inside the house. She had made it, after all this time. She was so close.

Flavia cried a little, to get that part over with, then pulled herself together and tidied her hair. "You can do this," she told the green reflection in the mirror. "Easy as dancing."

The next step was to meet the children.

Mindful that she was supposed to dress like a lady rather than a servant (though not too fine a lady), Flavia changed into her best acorn-brown dress. Her previous employers gave her the material in last year's Christmas box, and Flavia paid the local dressmaker to have it made up instead of muddling along herself with a needle that never did what it was told. The gown soothed her now, like a wet pond on a warm day.

Flavia had been taught the complicated rules of what was 'respectable' in society by her adopted aunt, a woman who thought respectability equated to godliness. Flavia had internalised all manner of ideas about modesty and a woman's lot long before she learned she was a fairy, born of a world where society and its rules were meaningless.

Green and trees and sweetness on your skin, whisper whisper, come to the dance, leaves and bark, dance all night, taste the berries, drink the water, laugh and sing, dance and dance, bare to the sky, hear the music in the wind and trees and leaves and kiss the grass, the twigs, breathe naked breathe kiss the girls dance dance breathe.

After Flavia turned twelve and the fairies appeared her dreams — the real fairies, the flesh and blood fairies, not the dear little toadstool variety — she found herself spilling over with questions. Why did no one ever ask aloud why Britannian women were restricted by corsetry and cotton in places that could not be seen, for the sake of presenting a certain womanly shape to the world? Why were some people seen as more important than others, automatically from birth, regardless of how well they could dance or stab or fly?

Why did mortals *never* challenge the unwritten rules of society that only seemed to become more oppressive with every passing year?

She must concentrate now. No distractions. Squashing down her fairy heritage, with all its impertinent questions, was a learned skill, and Flavia had made herself an expert. Strand by strand, she drew the green out of her hair, then her skin, until she looked like a Modest Governess again and not the wild dancing muddy creature who longed to escape these walls. The house was full of metal and rules and disapproving butlers, and she had to make the best of it, for now.

This was what the world saw when they looked at her: Flavia Wednesday, a young woman with a face plain enough that employers rarely worried she might catch the eye of their husbands. Her figure was what the mistresses at school referred to as 'sturdy' — wide shoulders and a solid waist that did not budge regardless of whether she starved herself on broth or stuffed her stomach with cakes. The skin and hair colour was a lie, but everything else about her was real.

Respectable. Flavia Wednesday always looked respectable. She had made an art form of respectability.

No one would guess her secrets.

The Gloucester children had three rooms on an upper floor, well away from any space that the adults might use on a daily basis. Flavia found her way along a twisting picture gallery, only to be glowered at by several generations of ancestor portraits in heavy oils.

What with the peaches and lemons drawing room, and her own cozy corner of the attic, she had almost forgotten how much the rest of this house disliked her. Still, not one of the dead Gloucester ancestors had a nearly-new day dress the colour of acorns, and so Flavia managed to survive their disapproval.

The door of the schoolroom had a bolt on it, allowing it to be locked from the outside. Flavia opened the door, and peered in to find a tidy room replete with desks, a reading couch, and a shelf filled with the sort of books grown ups consider 'improving' and children consider to be only good for chocking up wobbly furniture.

"Hello?" she called.

The room was empty of humans. A scruff of a

tabby cat stretched into the pool of autumn sunshine from the window.

Flavia walked across the floor, her shoes making a satisfying rap with every step. She looked down at the tabby, and narrowed her eyes. It had a shimmer to it, a peculiar wave of heat that didn't make sense for the size and shape of the animal. The animal it was pretending to be.

She leaned down and made a quick pinching gesture, like picking a berry off a bush. The magic unravelled, and the cat spun around with a yowl. He blurred, all tabby fur and hissing, and then a half-dressed boy with messy hair tumbled out of the blur and fell in a heap on the floor. "Owww," he complained.

"I suppose you think you're being funny," Flavia accused.

"It was jolly funny with our last nanny," the boy said without hint of shame. The Honourable Dash-mond, one presumed. He stretched out on the floor-boards and smiled up at her. "I jumped out of a cupboard and changed before her eyes. She screamed all over the place and hit me with a broom."

Flavia was starting to realise why Lady Carolinge had been so quick to hire her. "I'm not a nanny," she said. "I'm your governess."

"What's the difference?" the boy asked with a lazy shrug.

"The difference is that I can do this." She seized

him by the ear, and gave him a shake. He folded up into the shape of the cat again, with an alarmed mew. Flavia caught hold of the creature, opened the nearest toy cupboard, and popped him on a shelf with some dolls and soldiers.

"You can't do that," piped up a voice from the doorway. "You can't put my brother in a cupboard." The Honourable Petronella, of course. The girl wore a starchy apron and a bright striped dress that didn't suit her in the least. Her long dark hair was braided unevenly, and there was a rather expensive fountain pen sticking out of one of the braids.

"Why not?" Flavia asked, on the verge of closing the glass-fronted door.

"He'll change into mice and gnaw on the wood," said the elder sister. "Mama hates it when he does that. She says we can't have another cupboard this year, not when he's already eaten three."

Flavia considered Petronella's point. "Very well." She opened the door again, and allowed the cat to leap to his freedom. "I shall let you off this time with a warning, Dashmond," she told him. "But tomorrow, I shall purchase a cage for when you need to be taught a lesson. Do we understand each other?"

The cat rolled on the floor until he was a boy again, and sat up looking sulky. "You've a rotten idea about jokes," he complained.

"I think I shall survive," Flavia replied. She

frowned at the boy. "Where did that sailor suit come from? You weren't wearing it before."

Dashmond shrugged. "My clothes disappear when I change," he said. "Sometimes I don't get the right ones back."

"Fascinating," said Flavia, because it was, really. "I think we've discovered a topic for your first composition. I want to know all about the things you can do with your magic, and what goes wrong most often when you do it."

"Really?" said Dashmond, in awe.

"We've never had anyone who wanted to know about that sort of thing," said Petronella, suspicious. She had that in common with her mother.

"Then I got here just in time," said Flavia. "My name is Miss Wednesday. What shall I call you?"

"Tabby," said Dashmond with a cheeky grin.

"He's Dash," said Petronella. "My mother hates nick-names, so you'll have to be careful around her. I prefer Queenie, when we're alone."

"I don't blame you," said Flavia. "Petronella sounds like an unpleasant medicine. What can you do, Queenie?"

The girl met her eyes with a defiant streak that made Flavia rather like her. "Embroidery, mathematics, and magical philtres," she said clearly. "I have a knack for mixing chemical compounds. I plan to recreate my great-grandfather's lost secret formula and restore our family fortune."

"Excellent," said Flavia. She hadn't been aware that the Gloucester family fortune was in any way endangered, and filed this information away for later use. She knew about the formula, of course.

The late Earl of Shuttlesworth, father to the current Earl, was famous for creating an antidote to love philtres earlier in the century, bringing an end to an era of forced marriages and slapstick scandals in London society. Such things still went on, especially on the Continent, but the extremely expensive Love-Me-Not philtre meant that freedom from enchantment was at least possible for the wealthy and privileged. Given that they were the people who had access to love philtres in the first place, it mostly worked out for the best.

"Have you a laboratory for your work?" Flavia asked Queenie. "The proper tools and equipment?"

"You're not a real governess," interjected Dash. "You're a spark, aren't you?"

Flavia gave him a superior look, summoning up the authoritative spirit of every snooty housemistress she had ever faced in training college. "What a common word," she said, refusing to answer his question. "I wonder where you learned it."

In her personal household, as in public life, Queen Isolda openly embraced the Imperial Concept: she had several trusted and beloved advisors who hailed from all corners of her new Britannian Empire, regardless of the colour of their skin.

It may have been the Duke of Bath who discovered Messrs Orlando and Rinaldo Device in a humble orphanage, and absorbed the two young geniuses into the royal household at Buckingham Palace, but it was Queen Isolda's active and enthusiastic patronage that turned these infamous paragons of magical engineering into the most famous metallurmages of the century.

Whether the Device brothers truly deserved the Queen's trust is a question that must certainly be asked, given the scandal that later occurred.

— Prof. Eamonn Bendigo, Isoldan Britannia: A Deconstruction, 1956.

Chapter 2

In Which the Countryside is Perilous and Kent is not Gloucester

The Extraordinary and Miraculous Device Brothers spent the night in a barn, not for the first time.

Rinaldo awoke first, peeling hay from his sleep-damp face. He scratched at what passed for stubble on his chin. The Exotic Beard of Mystery he had been working on for some time was failing to eventuate, and it itched like crazy. He was already sufficiently exotic and mysterious for Britannian audiences, with his brown skin and dark eyes, but if he must condescend to the Far East act with turban and silk trousers, the least he was owed was a beard.

His brother Orlando snored deeply a few feet away, his head cushioned upon a pillow improvised from his best flameproof coat, rolled up in a padded ball. Rinaldo kicked him, because it made him feel better. His headache eased, though the taste of stale beer in his mouth did not. He kicked his brother again, for good measure.

"Arumpsdfpsdh," said Orlando in his sleep, and kicked back. A moment later, he did that irritating thing he always did: snapping his eyes open and leaping to his feet, fully awake like a clockwork automaton who had been switched on in a hurry. "Right. Where are we then? Breakfast?" He darted his head back and forth as he took in their surroundings, his black hair sticking up in all directions like a windswept scarecrow. The witch's ruby on its gilded chain spilled out of his shirt, and Orlando stuffed it back out of sight, doing up a button or two and patting his pockets to find his cravat. "Where are we, Professor?"

"Devonshire," said Rinaldo, stretching. Every muscle in his body twanged from the uncomfortable night, and his joints cracked here and there with little pops.

"What the hellfire are we doing in Devonshire?"

"Running away," sighed his brother. Orlando was useless in the mornings. It was like trying to talk to a dancing puppy. You wouldn't think they were practically the same age. Rinaldo had always looked at the world through the eyes of an adult, even as a child. Orlando was happily set in his ways as a callow youth and likely would remain unchanged at four score and ten, if he lived that long without being murdered by a cuckolded husband.

"Gotta piss," said Orlando, and lurched out of the barn.

"Don't let anyone see you," Rinaldo called after him. He stared mournfully at the pack they had dragged with them when they high-tailed it out of London. They barely had spare suits of clothes to their names, and only one top hat between them. So much for the Extraordinary and Miraculous Device Brothers. All of their stage kit was gone, left behind at the Mortmain witch's house in surety for their service. Including the turban and silk trousers, now he came to think of it.

Starting from scratch. They were paupers, just as they had been back in the orphanage before a kind Duke's patronage put them on the path to glory, fame, fortune and... now, ruin.

"That enchantress," muttered Orlando, bursting back in with his trousers askew. "Evil old trout. This is all her fault. You should never have let me go begging to her when it all went tits-up at the Palace."

"You didn't think she was an evil old trout a few days ago," Rinaldo retorted, with greater heat than he might have bothered to summon if his brother was entirely wrong. "You thought she was a beautiful silver-lined cloud, a snake-hipped vixen, and the answer to our prayers. Those are all direct quotes from your actual mouth."

"Obviously she slipped me a love philtre," his brother said airily.

"If only you'd stop letting your guard down around blondes," Rinaldo snorted. "She's old enough to be your mother."

"Good kisser," Orlando sighed. "But, yes. Evil traitorous, vixen-hipped witch." His eyes melted into fondness for a moment. "We should pledge ourselves to her eternally, as soon as we have fulfilled this quest," he declared in a voice not entirely his own. "I'm sure we have misunderstood that gracious lady's intentions. A lifetime in service to her would be an honour and a privilege..."

Rinaldo rummaged in the pack and pulled out a slim vial with only a precious half-inch of Love-Me-Not left inside. "Most valuable thing we own and you run through it like water," he complained, tossing it to Orlando. "That's our last, don't slurp it like buttermilk. One drop."

"Yes, Professor." Orlando pulled out the dropper and let a single drop of the antidote fall on his tongue, then screwed up his face as if he had taken poison. "Ugh, tastes like balls. Boiled balls."

"And what have we learned from this enterprise?" Rinaldo confiscated the vial back and tucked it away in the pack. "When mysterious magical women want something from you..."

"Don't drink the wine."

"Don't eat or drink *anything*."

Orlando nodded. "I think it was the violet creams this time. Noticed they had a tang of vervain."

"But you still ate three."

"They were delicious."

"You take that antidote for granted," Rinaldo complained. "One of these days you'll have to marry whichever woman pours a philtre into your tea when my back is turned."

Orlando grinned at him, utterly unrepentant. "Let us hope the future Mrs Device is rich and bouncy."

"Knowing your jammy luck," sighed his brother, "she probably will be."

~

Of course they were going to complete Lady Mortmain's quest. They had no choice. Not if they wanted to reclaim Orlando's lost magic, and hide from the wrath of the Queen of Britannia. Still, Rinaldo couldn't evade the worry that it was all too easy.

Rinaldo could always spot the trap. This was how he had managed to keep Orlando and himself alive so far. Well, mostly Orlando. His brother was the one who attracted deadly peril and magical temptresses like flies, while Rinaldo cleaned up the debris left in his wake.

After they evaded the angry sheep farmer who owned the barn, not to mention his many large sons who assumed that Rinaldo and Orlando were sheep thieves, the Device brothers made their way through the woods on foot for some hours before Rinaldo felt it safe to return to the public road.

"On to Gloucester," said Orlando, pointing in the wrong direction.

"Do you ever listen?" Rinaldo demanded. "We're not going to Gloucester. The family is *called* Gloucester, and their holding is in *Kent*."

"That's uncivilised confusing of them. We might have got lost."

"You might," his brother grumbled. "Luckily, I pay attention to whole sentences at a time. It's my special magic power. Kent is nearer to here than Gloucester, so consider us fortunate. Especially as you weren't pointing in the right direction for either."

Orlando looked pitiful. "Does that mean I shouldn't have paid sixpence for a map of Gloucestershire before we left London?"

Rinaldo rolled his eyes. "If you got it off Jimmy the Pigger, you shouldn't have paid sixpence under any circumstances. Don't you remember that Nottingham map that he sold you? He made up half the street names, and drew them in himself."

"It was a bargain at half price."

"Aye, that's the very definition of a bargain, paying half price for worthless."

They walked in silence for some time. If only it could always be that way.

"We should get a donkey," Orlando decided after a while. "If we're to do all this travelling."

"You are a donkey," muttered Rinaldo.

Orlando grinned at him. That was the worst thing about Rinaldo's brother: insults rolled off him like raindrops. "If I'm a donkey, I need better shoes."

~

Kent was the garden of England, it was said. Rinaldo reflected on this as he scraped the third cowpat of the day off the sole of his boot. Presumably, this was said by people who wanted to sell land in Kent, or needed to convince themselves that living outside a city was in any way civilised.

"Fine weather for crops, at least," he observed as he turned up the collar of his shirt to keep the drizzle from sliding down his neck.

"It's not growing season, Professor Brains-are-full," replied Orlando, who had disappeared from the road for a good hour or so to scrump apples, and now chewed through one with disgusting smacking noises. His pockets were laden, bulging out in all directions. "It's harvest time."

They had been on foot for days now, camping out in various barns and dodging farmers who had a litany of names to yell at tramps who looked like foreign devils. This was it, though: the village of Shuttlesworthing should be beyond this next hill. A good thing too. Rinaldo wasn't sure how long his boots would hold out, and he didn't fancy tromping through cowpats once the soles had split.

"So," Orlando said thoughtfully. "Any pretty ladies at the house? That we should investigate in order to avoid, of course," he added.

"None who are likely to seduce or enchant you in order to learn your secrets," said Rinaldo. "So not your type. There's only Lady Carolinge, our patron's sister, and the further we keep you away from her, the better. She's a harpy and a half, from what I hear, and she hates magic with a passion."

"Doesn't she find that inconvenient, with a famous enchantress like Lady Mortmain as a sister?" asked Orlando with his mouth full.

"I expect so."

The two young men came over the rise and gazed at the view. A pretty village sprawled out beneath them, the type that was often sketched in volumes of poetry or painted upon the sentimental Christmas cards that were all the rage in London.

"I see a pub!" Orlando declared in triumph.

"You don't get extra marks for that," Rinaldo said sourly. "We'll save money by sleeping in the woods."

"Who said anything about sleeping? I have drinking coin!"

Rinaldo patted his pockets and realised that his brother had stolen his purse. "Do that again and I'll see you in the stocks myself," he snapped, digging through Orlando's own pockets and retrieving three apples before he found the purse. "Or debtor's prison, see if I don't."

"You're a harsh man to deprive your beloved sibling of a drink. You know it makes sense to try the pub. We can listen for gossip about the manor."

Rinaldo sighed. It was better than any plan he had, and the idea of a bed for the night was a mighty temptation. "One drink," he said, knowing that Orlando would talk him into three. He had to pretend reluctance, for his dignity.

As they approached the pub, Rinaldo noticed a sign that they were hiring. "Look at that! We can earn our drink. All you have to do is cast aside your objection to honest work for a day or two."

Orlando groaned at the thought of it. "You and your respectability, Professor. Where's the fun in that?"

SPARK (noun): *a colloquialism referring to natural practitioners of magic, especially those of the lower classes: Metallurmagic, hearthcraft, flying and other small magics, along with those who utilise such powers, are often referred to as sparks, though never in polite company.*

Sparks (plural) can also refer to the practice and/or presence of magic itself, especially when used in an everyday or ordinary manner.

See: Enchanters *and* Sorcerers *for a higher class of magic practitioner. See:* Witch *for the lowest class of all.*

— The Encyclopedia of Magic, 1814 edition.

Chapter 3

In Which Toadstools Are False, Storybooks Are Essential, and a House has its Secrets

Flavia learned that magic was real when she was twelve years old. Before that, she thought it a silly concept, invented by old ladies who wrote dear little stories for children.

She was raised in a cottage by her adopted great-aunt, Primula Millicent Wednesday, a prominent author of stories about quaint toadstool fairies and the like. These tales were published in the Sunday newspapers as well as in beautifully-bound books with dainty watercolour illustrations.

Primula Millicent Wednesday painted her own pictures, though she made sure to regularly inform her great-niece that her little rose elves and acorn pixies were Not Based On Factual Observation.

Flavia's childhood had shaped her into an intensely skeptical young lady who preferred reading books about history and mathematics.

Then the voices started, and the dreams, around the time that she learned the womanly secrets for which Great-Aunt Primula had in no way prepared her (thank goodness for the eminently sensible widow Mrs Frock, who came in to do for them every morning, and knew a girl trying to hide blood-stained drawers when she saw one).

At first, Flavia could convince herself that her nightly adventures were born of an over-active imagination, and a cottage full of paintings of toadstools. She could dance in the wild woodland with naked creatures all wings and kisses and whispers, and still tell herself in the morning that the world was made of science and logic and reality.

Then, the magic started. Dried flowers became fresh when Flavia entered the room. Grass lay down before her to cushion her steps. Ivy coiled itself neatly around her wrists as if it wanted to bedeck her for a fairy tale ball. The garden fell halfway in love with her, and the nearby woods were even worse. Flavia once had to stay out after sunset because several tree roots had curl their branches lovingly around her waist and would not let go.

Then there was the girl in the mirror, the silver creature with the delicious voice who teased and promised and finally confessed all her secrets to Flavia. Quicksilver was her only friend. The first person in her life who told her the truth.

Great-Aunt Primula reacted badly to the idea that

her ward (not her niece or great-niece, as it turned out, not even a blood relation) was talking to fairies. The first time she caught Flavia sleeping outside, one hand lazily brushing against the branch of a walnut tree as if she had bid goodnight to a lover, the elderly lady arranged for the girl to be sent to the School of Good Wives and God's Mercy. Flavia was trained as a governess with the expectation that all thoughts of magic and wickedness would be beaten out of her, by sticks and straps if not by logic and schoolbooks.

It was too late for Flavia. She already knew that the place she visited in her dreams was real. She knew what it was like to run barefoot across that soft, magical grass. She knew that the silver girl in the green mask who gazed at her from every reflective surface was a flesh-and-bone friend who loved her and believed in her.

She knew that she had a real mother.

She knew her purpose.

Now, Flavia was so close to having everything she had always wanted. She was so close to completing the quest for which she was born.

She was counting the days. And in the meantime, she might as well be the best governess she could be for the magically-deprived Gloucester children.

Flavia settled in rather well with Queenie and Dash. The children were delighted to discover that she intended to teach them magic instead of merely showing them how to conceal it in public.

They did lessons in the morning: mathematics and history, literary compositions, Latin translation and French conversation. After lunch, the three of them would go for a brisk walk around the grounds before returning to the familiar grand edifice that was Gloucester Worth.

There were four gardens in total, hemmed in by hedges: 1) a rose arbour that was mercifully free of pixies (the first thing Flavia checked), 2) an ornamental maze, 3) a little wilderness and 4) a trimmed lawn for tennis and croquet. Each garden was expertly designed and maintained, down to the last blade of grass. Even the wilderness was a carefully controlled masterwork, with colour co-ordinated thistles and a matching pair of leafy bowers.

Here in the green and the leaves and the pollen-dusted air, Flavia could finally breathe, away from the house that (mostly) hated her. The daily walks kept her feeling alive. When she walked among the greenery, she always kept an eye on the space she knew was there: the archway to nowhere, so hidden by its sheer ordinary nature that no one would ever spot it.

Not unless they knew what to look for.

After the children returned to the house with their governess each afternoon, they would embark upon a lesson that Flavia called 'scientific method,' and Dash called 'sparks class.' The children did not have a laboratory as such, only a playroom furnished with the sort of toys suited to much younger children: rocking horses and wooden hoops. Queenie had set up a makeshift work space on a table too small for her where she worked intently on 'messes' of herbs, chemical compounds and exotic foreign ingredients.

Flavia took one look at all this, that first day, and set both children to clearing out the playroom. They moved the larger toys up to the attic, hiding them among a dusty heap of sea trunks, spare wardrobes and archived family treasures.

Two long benches gave Queenie a better space to work, while the rest of the room was left empty for Dashmond's experiments. The boy had a knack for metamorphosis — he could transform into a dozen different animals, though he preferred cats above all other shapes. It was several days before Flavia realised that he could only change into animals he had seen before – and that in most cases, he had only seen them in books, which explained why his zebra was the size of a small dog, and his elephant was oddly two-dimensional.

It was for the best to keep Queenie and Dash apart while they worked. The boy's wild transforming antics combined with his sister's delicate balance of liquids and glass vials were an industrial accident waiting to happen. Once Flavia helped them set up separate spaces, she noticed that Queenie became more free with her magic. The girl had a knack for glass as well as alchemical combinations, and was often to be seen transporting her philtres and test-portions around the makeshift laboratory in floating globes.

The book situation was a disgrace. Never mind the lack of reference works dealing with the magic that the family had ignored in their children for years, but there were barely even any storybooks. The majority of the texts available for Queenie and Dash in the schoolroom were basic lesson books, dull and lifeless.

A quiet investigation among the maids revealed that there was a library in the house, rarely used during the day though it was often visited by the gentlemen of the house after dinner, when they gathered for port and cigars.

Flavia made several discreet visits, choosing books that she thought would be useful for the children, and smuggling them back to the schoolroom. She discovered an alcove in the library full of fairy stories, and appropriated them for their intended audience.

On one of these expeditions she paused with her hand hovering over one particular book, wondering whether to add it to the stack or not. She had found it hidden behind a children's atlas, probably so that Lady Carolinge would not throw the thing out of the house due to her apparent dislike of toadstool stories and other 'nonsense' for children. *Acorn's Dear Little Tea Party* by Primula Millicent Wednesday. Oh, that one. Flavia remembered that one. Long nights of burning candles as Great-Aunt Primula tried to capture the dainty features of her protagonist, an elfin boy with diaphanous moth-shaped wings.

"The wings are wrong," Flavia had told Great-Aunt Primula quite by accident one evening. "They shouldn't be so round."

That memory brought others rushing forward, of the shrill and angry voice of her guardian. *"Harlot! Strumpet! I know where you go at night. I know what you do."*

She had never understood why Great-Aunt Primula thought the worst of her, why she assumed young Flavia was a fallen woman simply because she went sleepwalking a time or two, and tracked soft dirt into the cottage on the soles of her bare feet.

"Wicked creature, you've spoiled it, you spoiled it all!" The old woman snarled, a week before she wrote the letter to send Flavia away to school. *"They were innocent, my little darlings, and look at you, all legs and bosom, I know where you've been! I know who you've been kissing!'*

In the cool quiet of the library, Flavia touched her own cheek, feeling the heat there. She had blushed at that accusation, not through any genuine loss of virtue, but because of the truth behind her dreams — at fifteen years old she no longer dreamed of sweet little fairies like in her Great-Aunt's books.

The woodland dancers of her dreams had indeed become wanton and lush creatures, as like to kiss you with teeth and tongue as to laugh at you for not knowing the steps to the dance. Every night Flavia returned to them in her dreams, and found herself tugged at and teased, pulled this way and that to the music.

She felt beautiful, there, in a way she never felt beautiful in the mortal world. And yes, she had been kissed, by all manner of magical creatures who were anything but sweet and innocent.

How had the elderly Miss Primula Millicent Wednesday guessed at such a truth?

Flavia's thoughts were interrupted now by an aristocratic male voice, deep and assured. "Perrault, is that you?" drawled Lord Salisbury.

Flavia froze with the children's books clutched to her chest. Bad enough to be caught in here by that snooty butler. One of the family was far worse.

She was thinking like a servant already. Her true mother would be... well. Disappointed hardly covered it.

As often happened when she was startled or worried, Flavia felt the green coming out in her, and had to shove it back down inside her skin. *It hardly counts as camouflage indoors, you ridiculous body.* She concentrated her magic on being small, oh so quiet, hardly worth noticing. The maids often used such techniques to avoid being seen, though they relied on social embarrassment and the traditions of class rather than magic.

A tall figure in a long coat swept past her alcove, and somehow the lamp between them served to keep Flavia hidden.

"You found me," said another voice, sounding somewhat abashed. "I'm hiding from your wife, Salisbury. She wants to talk about suitable young ladies again, and I don't dare break ranks to tell her what I really think."

"Gad, no," said the father of Flavia's young charges. "Can't have that, man. She wouldn't be liveable with. But I have to suffer the consequences, don't you know."

Perrault laughed in a low voice. "I suppose you had to marry her..."

The elder brother smacked the younger, a light gesture to show there was no true insult taken. "None of that cheek."

Flavia felt an odd sense of outrage on behalf of the unseen Lady Carolinge whom, it had to be said, was easier to like when she wasn't in the room. Lord Salisbury's wife was the exact opposite of the nag that they joked about. The lovesick lady treated her thoughtless husband as if he walked on water.

"I've had a letter from Elspeth," Lord Salisbury went on. "Father is pressing for us to visit London. The lawyers are circling like buzzards, and the creditors aren't far behind. Can't leave Elspeth to deal with it all, isn't done for a woman to discuss financials. And Father is being difficult again."

The younger brother was unsettled by this revelation. "Filthy business," he muttered. "I suppose we must. The household will be at sixes and sevens, though. You know what servants are like. And we can't both go, not at this time of year. Someone must stay with the garden until the damned Hallows is past."

"I'll put it off," said Salisbury. "There's a village do that night. They'll expect the lord of the manor to show his face, and Carolinge has signed us up for dinner with the Postlethwaites afterwards."

"Will Father be able wait until November?"

"He'll have to. I'm sure Elspeth is exaggerating the troubles."

"Wouldn't be so bad if we could travel by the blessed train," sighed Lord Perrault.

The two men left the library, muttering amongst themselves. Flavia remained for a few moments, before gathering her new treasures and returning to the nursery.

The words, 'someone must stay with the garden' were trapped in her head, repeating like a music hall chorus. They knew about the garden. *They knew*. That could make her task harder.

◠

Flavia enjoyed her time at Gloucester Worth. The children were bright and eager, flowering like apple blossom under the sunlight of her encouragement. Even Lady Carolinge was pleased with their behaviour on the rare occasion that she took notice of the children at all.

Many a time, when Flavia brought the children to say goodnight to their mother and father, Lady Carolinge ignored them entirely or sent them away without a word. Only when her husband was not present did she kiss them, or ask if they had been good. It was... unsettling, how much she doted upon her husband above all else.

Lord Salisbury himself never asked the children anything about themselves. He might occasionally rap out a demand for Dashmond to recite his times table, but that was not the same as showing a personal interest in the boy. Petronella was the subject of the occasional mild jest about finding husbands, but otherwise abandoned to her own devices.

It was still better than Flavia's last placement, where the mother constantly interfered in the lives of her daughters. Queenie and Dashmond were acceptable company, and did not display any overt distress at their neglect.

Two weeks passed quickly. If she was not careful, Flavia might become so comfortable here that she would not be able to do what was necessary.

She ate meals with the children, and had limited interaction with the rest of the staff. Occasionally, in the evenings, she made a point of visiting the servants hall so as not to appear aloof. She knew from past experience that it was best not to give anyone a reason to dislike you.

The downstairs household was every bit the emotional battlefield as upstairs, only with a larger ensemble. The maids and footmen, supervised by Mrs Holloway the housekeeper, were engaged in a silent war against the kitchen staff, with Mrs Dawes the cook as their general. Mrs Dawes was a vengeful, angular sort of woman, quite the skinniest cook that Flavia had ever met.

Mr Graves the butler was the master of judgmental facial expressions. He allowed the household to orbit around him for the most part unless something displeasing crossed his path. He would leap upon said anomaly like a spider on its prey, feeding until there was nothing left but perfect clockwork routine.

The maids were all named Susan, except for the under house parlour maid, a cheery soul with red hair who was far too junior to have been asked yet to surrender the name of Mavis. The footmen were both called William, again for the convenience of the family who could not be expected to remember two names when one would suffice. Both Williams had been hired to match in height, hair colour and general appearance, so Flavia had to concede that the naming system was practical. It was a relief not to have to try to tell them apart.

Everything about working in service was practical, with no room for sentiment. Flavia limited her time in the servants hall as much as she could, because she found their company so very depressing.

She could not avoid Mavis, who was ridiculously sweet and merry, and regularly sneaked up to the nursery to insist that Flavia join them for a mug of cocoa and a chinwag. Mavis was fascinated that Flavia had once lived in London, a place she seemed to think was paved with gold and glazed with sugar.

"Don't you join the family when they go up to town?" Flavia asked aloud at the table, one evening in the servants hall.

They stared at her, aghast. Not only Mavis, but the Susans and the Williams too. Mrs Dawes and Mrs Holloway the housekeeper were for once completely in sympathy with each other, gaping in equal horror, while Mr Graves mopped his mouth diligently with a cloth napkin to hide his evident distress.

"Go up there?" said Mavis finally. "Ooh. As if we would."

"The London house has its own staff," said Mr Graves. "My own father, Mr Graves Senior, is the butler at Number 12 Actaeon Place, and performs his duty to a greater standard than I could ever hope to accomplish in this lifetime. I strive at all times to aspire to his excellence."

There was a moment's silence as everyone absorbed the fact that the elderly and venomously perfectionist Mr Graves had a father still living, whom he considered a superior butler.

"Is that usual?" asked Flavia, knowing herself to be on shaky ground, but unable to resist another dig. "At my last house, several of the servants travelled with the family, wherever they went."

"The servants of Gloucester Worth do not leave Gloucester Worth," said Mr Graves. "Not under any circumstance." He looked ill at the idea.

Flavia was tempted to make a joke about half days off to lighten the mood, but the expressions on all of their faces made it very clear that such levity would not be welcomed.

Loneliness washed over her. She held tightly on to that feeling. Making connections here – learning to understand or even to like these people – none of that was necessary. She was not one of them. She was not even of the same species.

So why did she keep trying?

"Do you visit London?" Flavia asked Queenie the next morning, while fixing the young girl's hair. She had taken over this task because Queenie, left to her own devices, was likely to get distracted halfway through braiding and end up tangled in a curtain cord, or woven into a chair with a stray ribbon. The girl was a genius at the brewing of philtres, but she hadn't the head for everyday chores.

"Oh yes," said Queenie. "Aunt Elspeth summons us a few times a year."

That was an odd way to phrase it. "Do you mean, she invites you?"

"Not really, no. It's fun in London. There are several museums. And the Crystal Palace is the centre of scientific know-how."

"And the centre of magical learning as well, of course," said Flavia.

The girl shrugged. "I suppose."

The children were trained to leave such things unspoken, as if magic was a matter of which to be ashamed. Was this embarrassment a Gloucester family tradition, or did it stem purely from Lady Carolinge?

What little Flavia had gleaned of the children's history suggested that none of their previous nannies had any talent for sparks or philtres, chosen instead for skills in discipline, sock-mending and copperplate handwriting. It beggared belief that a family of such extreme privilege should have been so irresponsible with the welfare and education of two highly talented children for so long.

The house itself was low in magical vibrations, apart from those provided by Queenie and Dash themselves. It was a rare old Britannian house to have survived so many centuries without acquiring a single ghost, cursed walkway, or far-too-secret-door.

Still, there was *something* here. Flavia had not dreamed of Faerie, not a single night since she set foot in this place. She did not see visions of Quicksilver or the other fairies, not in the reflection of a mirror or a puddle in the gardens. Not anywhere within the walls or hedges of this home. She had never felt so isolated in her life. How had the Gloucesters managed such protections? Was it due to the proximity of the gate in the garden, the one she only ever saw in the corner of her eye?

Flavia could not get caught up in wondering about the secrets of Gloucester Worth. On All Hallows Eve, she would be finally reunited with her mother and her friend, and she could be green, and green, and *green*. No more pretence. No more loneliness. No more humans.

Home. It was so close she could nearly taste it.

If Flavia felt guilt at all, it came in tiny pangs, easily squashed and ignored.

~

Dash took to the new books with relish, especially the storybooks. The fairy tales had an unfortunate side effect in that they introduced him to the concept of dragons. It was only quick thinking on Flavia's part and the judicious application of a bucket of bathwater that saved the curtains from his flaming breath. She had to move several rugs around to disguise what had been done to the schoolroom floorboards once Dash returned to being a shamefaced but secretly delighted young human boy.

Flavia visited the library several times more to abduct works by Mr Robert Louis Stevenson, Mr Rudyard Kipling, Mr L. Rider Haggard and Mr. Aesop, in order to fuel the boy's interest in reading as well as to encourage him to practice the shapes of animals other than monsters.

Queenie scorned all fiction. Nor was she remotely interested in factual texts concerning mythology, history or magic, unless they referred to the brewing of philtres and other sciences. "I don't have time for fripperies," she said, tossing her braids.

"Some people read for pleasure as well as information," Flavia suggested.

"Some people don't need to make a scientific breakthrough before they are old enough to come out in society," Queenie retorted, and returned to her test tubes.

A GENTLEWOMAN'S GUIDE TO LOVE PHILTRES

It is known that a young lady of attractive face and substantial dowry must constantly guard against fortune-hunters armed with love philtres. Be alert! One drop in your tea can make you lose every ounce of good sense or self-preservation.

Guard your virtue and your dowry, young gentlewomen, by following these simple steps:

1) Never accept a drink from a gentleman, even if he is known to your family. Likewise, be cautious about cups presented to you by sisters of impoverished gentlemen, or servants who might be vulnerable to bribes. The current fashion for ladies to serve themselves punch from a shared bowl exists for a reason — make use of it!

2) Be cautious of any gentleman seeking to share refreshment with you alone. Love philtres

depend on whom you first see after consumption. It is unlikely that a true fortune-hunter should offer you a dose in mixed company, for fear you might fall in love with the footman.

3) We are all gentlewomen here, and so I would be remiss in not confessing an uncommonly-discussed fact about love philtres: should you take one by accident, it is not only gentlemen who are like to become the apple of your eye. Do not assume you are safe in the company of your fellow ladies.

4) Thanks to our hero Mr Richard Gloucester: toast of the ton, alchemist extraordinaire and soon (it is rumoured) to be made Britannia's newest Earl, it is possible for any lady to equip herself with an invaluable tonic known as 'Love-Me-Not.' This is not a preventative for involuntary affection, but can be used to cure a love philtre after the fact.

5) Upon consuming a love philtre, you are the person least likely to notice. This is where our companions and sisters are essential to our survival. If a young marriageable lady of your acquaintance becomes overwrought or is rendered insensible by an unexpected romantic attachment, be prepared to share your vial of Love-Me-Not — and make sure that other

young women of your acquaintance are
prepared to do the same.

6) A single drop of Love-Me-Not can be
discreetly administered via a cup of tea or upon
a lump of sugar, if the subject is recalcitrant.
Check with a doctor or alchemist within twelve
hours if symptoms persist.

— Instructional pamphlet distributed to
young ladies of Society, Britannia
(1817). Reprinted due to high demand
in 1819, 1820, 1823, 1824 and four
times in 1827.

Chapter 4

In Which the Empress of Catapults is Formally Introduced to Mr Orlando Device, Esquire

Flavia spent her half-day in the village, purchasing pen wipers for herself and writing paper for Queenie, who had a birthday coming up and many thank you notes ahead of her. There was a small budget allowed for schoolroom expenses, but Flavia had already spent it replacing items destroyed by Dash during his transformations.

When the family headed to London, she might finally be able to acquire a new Latin dictionary for the children, as the only one they had was illustrated and heavily abridged. Still, that would require a conversation with Lady Carolinge, and Flavia had not yet worked up the courage.

It was a ridiculous thought. The London trip was planned for after All Hallows, and she would no longer be here. Flavia could not afford to forget that this job was temporary.

Mavis, the under house parlourmaid, accompanied Flavia around the shops all morning with her cheery chatter. Now, she was supposed to meet her young man in the tea room. Mavis had become quite beside herself with worrying what people might say, and whether anyone might blab to Mrs Holloway that she had a follower. Flavia offered to sit at a nearby table, to keep the young couple company without being a complete gooseberry, but apparently that was not the done thing either.

Great Aunt Primula Millicent had taught Flavia a great many rules and behaviours concerning respectability, but when Flavia was sent away to school she learned that many of them were quite wrong, especially for a 'big house'. What was acceptable for a schoolgirl and her unworldly maiden aunt in a rustic village was completely at odds with what was acceptable for a female servant. The rules concerning Young Ladies of Quality were different again.

No one seemed to have a complete handle on the rules of Appropriate Respectability for a governess, given their in-between status, but oh, *everyone* would notice if she got it wrong. It was like constantly standing on the edge of a cliff, balancing in a full corset and petticoats, waiting for someone to throw a book of Ladylike Behaviour at your head.

Life was so much easier for fairies. No one cared about respectable in the greenwood. Flavia's long nights dreaming herself into their world, dancing the dances and laughing with the merry creatures had meant that by the time she was sent to the School of Good Wives and God's Mercy, her Great Aunt's teachings held little sway over her.

More than once, she would say something quite by accident that others thought was scandalous.

It was ridiculous, how humans thought you could police people's ideas as easily as their bodies. Surely, the whole point of confining young unmarried ladies with stiffly corseted underthings was to prevent wickedness regardless of what went on in their heads.

After offering several sensible solutions to Mavis' tea room conundrum, Flavia finally came to the conclusion that the fretting about getting into trouble was an essential ingredient of the romantic assignation. Relieved, she left Mavis in good conscience, promising to be back in an hour so they could walk back to the big house together, so no one (except, presumably, the entire village and anyone who travelled through it today) should be any the wiser.

Mortals were so very complicated.

As she crossed the square, Flavia noticed that a crowd had gathered, laughing and jeering at an entertainment. Many held tankards or half-eaten pies from the local beer house. Curious, Flavia joined them.

The first thing she noticed was a young Chinese gentleman kneeling in the stocks, his head and hands locked into the simple but ruthless device. He appeared to be entirely unbothered by his predicament, laughing and joking despite the crushed fruit smeared into his wild black hair.

Concerned, Flavia looked to the crowd, who were crowded around a young man who was also of Eastern appearance, possibly from Her Majesty's Empire of India.

This Indian gentleman was in greater favour than the Chinese fellow in the stocks. The villagers fell over themselves to pat him on the back and shove all manner of items into his hands: metal mostly, old clocks, broken tools, the sort of detritus one might find behind a blacksmith's hovel, or in cellars across the country. The gentleman, with great determination, set about assembling the broken pieces into something marvellous.

'Spark' was a slang term for any type of magic except the brewing of magical philtres, which were regarded as a separate and more scientific discipline. But this young man's particular knack, Flavia realised, was for the magical field from which the term originated. He was a builder of extraordinary devices: a metallurmage.

Every piece of metal handed to the gentleman — every lever or clock hand or wheel spoke — he braided into an artful tangle that whirred and hummed beneath his touch as if it was already a working engine. His hands moved so fast that they blurred, and a contraption of great beauty emerged from his quick fingers amid the creak of metal and hum of power from his fingertips.

Flavia had always known that magic like this existed in the world, but fairies had a natural dislike of metal – of iron especially – and so she had never watched metallurmagic performed. The presence of so much iron made her skin itchy and uncomfortable, but there were other metals here (bronze and copper and brass) which did not bother her at all.

The work was fascinating, as the metallurmage formed levers and limbs with his hands. It was worth a little discomfort to see a miracle take shape so easily before her eyes. There was nothing Flavia liked so well as competence: to watch a master perform his skill with refined technique.

When the device was complete, the performer revealed it with a flourish. The crowd burst forth into great laughter. The Chinese gentleman in the stocks laughed along with them at the sight of such a splendid machine.

It was a catapult. A veritable empress of catapults. This beautiful device had no less than eight different arms, each of which could be loaded with a touch, and fired with a combination of sounds such as clicking fingers, a belch, or a clap of the hands. The villagers contributed the scraps of their luncheons with great enthusiasm and watched as the young metallurmage clapped, whistled and clicked the right combination to send every arm juddering into the air, showering the

Chinese gentleman in the stocks with beer, pie crust, apricots and some rather soft-cooked turnip gruel.

Was this cruelty or entertainment? Flavia was not quite sure, but the villagers accepted it with joy. The local blacksmith slapped the metallurmage on the back, and shook the hand of the very sticky young man in the stocks. The blacksmith then took possession of the new catapult and wheeled it away, with most of the village following in an atmosphere of great merriment.

The two young gentlemen remained in the square with only Flavia watching. The metallurmage began to unlatch the stocks, allowing his messy compatriot to be released.

"Do you need any assistance?" she asked, feeling sympathetic to them. "I mean — in cleaning up, I suppose?"

The man from the stocks gave her a wide grin and the metallurmage promptly leaned over and stuck an apple in the fellow's mouth, to stop him talking. "That's nice of you, miss," he said politely. "But my brother Orlando here can sluice himself off behind the pub. We've managed to keep our jobs pulling pints, at least. For now," he added, with a stern look at the fellow he said was his brother.

Flavia should probably not be speaking to them like this, on a public street. It was one of those 'not the done things' that could earn her a scandalous reputation. Great Aunt Primula Millicent had never ventured an opinion on foreigners — did not even like to acknowledge that countries outside Britannia existed — and yet Flavia knew from her time in London that people of dark complexion were viewed with an undue amount of suspicion and ill feeling in some quarters. She had always taken this as a warning of how Britannians might respond to a green-skinned fairy walking among them.

Still, she only had a few more days before she would leave Gloucester Worth and the mortal world behind forever. Surely she could risk it, to have an intelligent conversation with a gentleman who created miracles.

"That device you built," she said, a questioning tone in her voice.

"Payment for a debt of honour," said the Indian metallurmage in a perfect, plummy London accent, more Upstairs than Downstairs. His smile was mostly in his eyes – kind eyes, Flavia thought. "Fast talking and bribery comes in handy with a reckless brother such as mine. That catapult is likely to fall apart within a month or so, but we should be well away from here by then."

Flavia thought of Dash and his keen interest in sparks. "I have a young student who would love to see your work," she said, before she could help herself.

The messy one, Orlando, spat out his apple and bowed at her with a charming smile that belied his food-strewn appearance. "We'll be performing at the

All Hallows fair, miss, if you've a mind to bring your lad along to see us."

"Rinaldo Device," said the other, holding out a hand quickly for Flavia to shake, as if he was afraid his brother might try to touch her and get onion pie all over her sleeves. "We're, ah. The Extraordinary and Miraculous Device Brothers." He had the grace to look mildly embarrassed by their grandiose title.

Out of the corner of her eye, Flavia saw Mavis staring at her through the tea shop window, eyes wide like saucers. Annoyed, Flavia took Mr Rinaldo Device's hand and shook it with genteel restraint. "Miss Wednesday," she said, returning his name with her own. The fair. She hadn't thought about the All Hallows fair. The children would howl to attend, and it fitted in with what she needed to do later that night – rather too well, as it happened. "I'll bring the children to see you at the fair."

"Hope so," Orlando Device said with a wicked grin, not helped by the layer of squashed turnip that still clung to his face. "Tell your friends."

Flavia bobbed her head politely and hurried away from the two gentlemen before she could cause further scandal, according to the standards of maids and butlers.

～

Queenie's thirteenth birthday was two days before All Hallows. Instead of breakfasting in the schoolroom, the children and Flavia were invited to join the Gloucester adults in the dining room. This involved a great deal of stilted and awkward conversation.

Lady Carolinge, besotted as ever with her husband, fussed around him endlessly at the breakfast. Mr Perrault Gloucester, Lord Salisbury's younger brother, lounged in his chair and looked bored, after coming up trumps with a telescope for Queenie's birthday present.

Queenie also received a string of pearls from her father, a family brooch from her mother, and a fur muff from her unseen Aunt Elspeth in London. Dash had conspired with Flavia to provide a set of new glass test tubes that were received with a more genuine smile than all the other gifts put together.

After the gentlemen excused themselves from the table, Lady Carolinge clapped her hands and insisted that Queenie (or Petronella, rather, as she was to her family) come upstairs to see her final birthday surprise. Flavia trailed along with Dash, both of them practicing quietness. After several years of causing noisy disruptions, young Dashmond had gleefully taken to the idea that he could get away with far more if no one saw or heard his mischief. He often begged Flavia to help him practice the art of what she called 'reasonable discretion' and he called 'spying'.

Dash's attempts at spying/discretion were all for naught today, as he fell about in fits of noisy laughter when he saw his mother's surprise for Queenie. No number of humbugs from Flavia's pockets would shut him up.

Queenie stood frozen in shock.

It was a bedroom. A lady's bedroom designed by someone who did not have the least idea as to Queenie's character. Lady Carolinge had ordered the best; that was clear. Quite why 'the best' had to all be in those particular shades of rose and peach, with quite so many ruffles, was a question for another day.

It was a china shepherdess of a bedroom. Everything flounced, from the curtains on the four-poster bed to the skirts of every leg belonging to the chairs, dressing table or lampshade. For each flounce, there was a ribbon in rose or peach, tied in a self-satisfied bow. Where there were ribbons, there were also tiny bells that caught the breeze and filled the air with a girlish tinkling sound.

"You're a young lady now," said Lady Carolinge, assuming her daughter's stunned silence to be gratitude. "Time you had a room of your own, while we consider your future."

Queenie's mouth snapped shut at that. "Am I to leave the nursery?"

Dash stopped laughing instantly. "You're taking Queenie away?"

"Only one floor up," said his mother, flustered by their rebellion. Flavia had no idea what reaction she had expected. "You're quite old enough to sleep on your own, Dashmond."

"I'm only seven," he said, and burst into tears.

Lady Carolinge looked from one child to the other. Queenie did not cry, but she looked thunderstruck. There would be no more creeping out first thing in the morning to check on her brewing philtres, or waking herself at midnight to capture exactly the right type of dew from the grass in the back garden. This room was on the same floor as her parents and uncle, hemming her in on all sides.

"Well," said Lady Carolinge finally. "I thought you would be pleased, Petronella. You're growing up."

"Yes," said Queenie in a soft voice. "I know I am."

"Not fair," Dash howled, and Flavia hauled him away by his ear. It seemed unlikely that he would calm down in the presence of all those ruffles.

As she left, she caught sight of Queenie kissing her mother's cheek, doing her best to look pleased. *Clever chicken*, Flavia thought silently. *You never get what you want by making a fuss.*

If Queenie really did want to escape all this, well. That made Flavia's job easier.

"But have you seen Fairy Tiptoe?" asked Shenanigan the leprechaun, taking a dainty bite out of his speckled toadstool. "None of us may proceed without her advice, begorrah."

The lovely fairy with the sapphire slippers appeared by magic.

"My word," said Fanny, blinking happy tears out of her eyes.

"With a swirl of my fairy wand, I shall show you anything you desire," declared the beauteous Fairy Tiptoe. "What do you most wish to see?"

"Might we visit someplace in past history?" requested Quentin. "A castle under siege, or maybe a pirate ship!"

"I should very much like to see a real queen," said Fanny. "Mayn't we visit the court of Good Queen Bess?"

A shadow passed across the face of Fairy Tiptoe. "Indeed I cannot take you there," she said. "Queen Bess of Britannia is an enemy to all fairykind. If she catches me, she will banish me into a bottle to live out my days alone forever."

"Oh bother," said Fanny. "Well, then. A pirate ship would be ever so jolly."

— *Fairy Tiptoe's Dear Little Wishes* (1860), written and illustrated by Primula Millicent Wednesday

Chapter 5

In Which the Crime of the Century is Interrupted by a Garden

Flavia could not eat a bite on the morning of the All Hallows fair. She fussed around the children's breakfast instead, which made them irritable.

She saw to their clothes, making sure that Dash wore the gentlemanly walking suit that his mother liked best. Flavia had to retie his cravat at least four times, as he wriggled out of it whenever her back was turned.

She helped Queenie into a day dress of sprigged yellow lawn which should be particularly pleasing to Lady Carolinge, though anyone else could plainly see that it made the poor girl look as though she had been dipped in mustard.

Sacrifices must be made.

Most of the servants were allowed an extra half-day, to enjoy the festivities. Flavia felt like a heel when the master and mistress of the house expressed their formal thanks that she had sacrificed her own holiday to supervise the children.

Dash gabbled away nineteen-to-the-dozen as they walked down to the village. He was excited about getting to see the Extraordinary and Miraculous Device Brothers, not to mention the whole day of sweets and rampaging which unfurled before him.

Queenie pretended to be ladylike and aloof about the whole affair, but Flavia knew that the girl was desperate to poke her nose into the alchemy tent and see which village brewers had won ribbons this year, since she herself was forbidden by her mother from entering.

I can let them have this day, Flavia thought fiercely to herself. *This last day.*

~

S he did not have to look very hard, to find the Extraordinary and Miraculous Device Brothers. A lopsided and badly spelled banner twisted in the trees above their heads. The two magical gentlemen stood apart from the village green, outside the main ring of the usual stalls and entertainments. Flavia was not sure if this was because they were unwelcome to join the other stalls or out of their own consideration for the safety of the villagers if there were likely to be explosions.

A crowd had gathered.

Mr Rinaldo Device the metallurmage had already constructed an outlandish contraption, far more complex than the Empress of Catapults. Dash's eyes glowed feline amber with delight as he beheld the machine. Flavia seized his collar before he could live up to his name. "Remember to be human," she whispered. The boy nodded, straightened his collar, and then ran full pelt towards the Device Brothers and their Extraordinary and Miraculous ... well.

It was a man. Not truly a man, for there was no life in those eyes, but the device had been built in the very shape of a man, down to a frock coat and high top hat. Every piece except the hat was metal. Like the catapult, Flavia could see that this mechanical man was made from scraps and oddments: bronze spoons and steel rods and iron scraps all woven together with miraculous skill.

In response to verbal instructions from both gentlemen, the automaton saluted the audience, doffed its hat with creaks and squeaks, bowed, and then waggled its head.

Flavia became aware that Queenie Gloucester remained at her elbow, standing very still. The girl watched the metal creature perform its tricks with a wary distrust.

"Is something wrong?" Flavia asked.

"I don't like it," said the girl after a moment's

thought. "There is something sinister to that creature. It's not real."

"I rather think that's the point," said Flavia, but she didn't dismiss the girl's caution. It was important that Queenie grew up learning to trust her own instincts. Besides, Flavia was also unsettled by the automaton, not only because there was so much iron incorporated into its being. This device was the opposite of every-thing that she knew to be good and natural and magical.

It did not grow. It did not live.

Her people would hate it. Her mother would condemn it as a miserable product of humankind — as an abomination.

But Flavia could not take her eyes off the mechan-ical man. If she ever needed something to stand between herself and the fairy folk, she would choose a guardian such as this one.

Where had that thought come from? The fairies would never hurt her. She was their hero. Their saviour.

Flavia would have liked to move on, pretending interest in jam or marrows or some more prosaic aspect of the village fair, but Dash had squeezed himself to the front of the crowd. She could not dislodge him now.

"Run on to the lemonade stall. I shall join you when I have secured your brother," she told Queenie, and noted the look of relief on her charge's face.

By the time Flavia made her way to Dash's side, the demonstration had come to an end and the crowd had partly dispersed. She found the boy pestering the gentlemen about their creation. Dash was eager to hear about the use of springs and oil, and not the least disappointed to learn that there were engineering practicalities at work in the automaton. The 'science of miracles' did not rely purely on sparks.

The boy's disinterest in anything that did not involve magic had been the bane of Flavia's life, these last few weeks.

"I do apologise if Master Gloucester has been at all impertinent," Flavia said as she approached. Mr Rinaldo Device smiled warmly. His wild-haired brother was far too caught up in an animated demonstration of levers to even notice her presence. "I'll bring him away if he's a bother."

"Don't worry about us," said Rinaldo, reclaiming the top hat from the automaton to place upon his own head. "Orlando loves a keen audience, especially if they're not throwing tomatoes. He might talk to your lad for days if we let him."

Flavia covered a smile with her hand. She was allowing herself to become distracted, and that was a risk to her mission, but at least it settled the nervous butterflies in her stomach. "Did you build this mechanical man?" she asked. "As you did your remarkable catapult? You're quite an inventor."

"I prefer the term *ingenieur*," Rinaldo said, in a

lofty voice, stressing a French accent on the word rather than the more prosaic 'engineer' which seemed a better everyday noun by far.

Flavia managed not to laugh at him. He had created a mechanical man. He was due a certain amount of pomposity.

"Miss Wednesday," said Orlando Device, finally breaking away from Dash's clutches to proffer her his hand. It was mercifully cleaner than it had been at their last meeting. "You came all this way to see our work again? We're honoured." He wore a neat brown suit, only slightly frayed at one cuff, with a watch chain hanging from his jacket and a gleaming red jewel on a chain at his throat. His black hair had been flattened with a brush on one side, which did little to tame its overall wildness.

He was ridiculously beautiful. This fact had been lost in all the squashed vegetables in his hair upon their first meeting, but it was impossible to ignore now. Flavia was quite used to beauty — mortals rarely offered any competition to her fairy friends in this regard — but Orlando Device was still a shock to her when he met her eyes and smiled with all his charm. Light practically shone from his eyes and teeth.

The entire experience was uncomfortable.

"Hardly a distance," said Flavia, shaking Orlando's hand, then stepping back so as to avoid any appearance of intimacy. "We are from the big house on the hill.

And Master Gloucester has always had a fascination for novelties."

"But can you make it go BOOM?" Dash whined, hanging off Orlando Device's leg in a puppyish fashion.

"Only on Sundays," said the pretty fellow with another of those charming smiles that lit up the village from end to end.

Flavia caught the grimace that Rinaldo sent in his brother's direction. *How much does Orlando Device get away with, wearing a smile like that?* she wondered, glad she was not his governess.

"We must be going," she said, but Dash wheedled another few minutes out of her. She stood in awkward companionship with the polite Rinaldo while his brother demonstrated the water jets that burst out of the mouth of the automaton, if one remembered to fill a small tank in its belly. The crowd loved that, and began to gather around them again, calling for more tricks.

"Your brother is good with children," Flavia ventured.

"Indeed," said Rinaldo. "He finds them less dull than grown ups, I think." Then, embarrassed, he added all in a rush: "Not that present company is dull, of course!"

"Oh, I am," said Flavia, turning her attention back to the automaton, and the look of joy on young Dash's face. "Frightfully dull."

Being interesting was the last thing she wanted, especially where gentlemen were concerned.

"Are you really brothers?" she asked without considering the consequences of the question.

Rinaldo's face closed over defensively. "Why would you ask that?"

Flavia hesitated. She shouldn't have said anything at all — should not have shown an interest. And yet, she always felt such indulgent kinship to those who were seen as outsiders in this formal world of Britannian society.

"Forgive me for being indelicate," she said after a fleeting war with her own thoughts. "You both seem quite different." Too late, she realised he might mean she was calling attention to their contrasting racial heritage and not, well. The way they walked through the world. One of them was calm and practical, the other dazzling with a strange, chaotic charisma.

"We were both born in Britannia," said Rinaldo, his voice cooler than before. Flavia had offended him, and should take that as her cue to leave.

After tonight none of this will matter.

And yet she did not want him to think ill of her. "I meant no offence," she said. "I am not, as it happens, entirely... Britannian. Your ways are still odd to me, sometimes."

Rinaldo's mouth twisted for a moment, caught up with his own internal thoughts. To Flavia's surprise, she saw something almost like humour in his deep brown eyes. He might not have the dramatic beauty of his brother, but he was a very presentable gentleman,. "People see what they expect to see," he said. "Don't you find?"

Oh, yes. She relied on that particular defence mechanism herself, every day.

"I've never quite believed in the motto that one can't choose your family," he added. "The world might be a less tumultuous place if that were true for everyone."

"I wouldn't know," said Flavia, a little taken aback by his certainty. She'd never been chosen by anyone, here in the mortal world. Quite the opposite. All she had was a disapproving great-aunt and a series of positions in other people's houses, taking care of children that were not her own.

I'll be with my real family soon. Finally, I will belong somewhere.

Dash was enraptured by the automaton's antics, clapping and laughing with merriment. Flavia called him away from Orlando with a clipped voice. "We must move on," she told the lad, despite his whines of disappointment. "I can't see your sister anywhere."

"Another time, perhaps, Miss Wednesday," said Rinaldo Device, raising his hat to her.

Flavia nodded politely, not wanting to encourage him. It was so complicated, the interactions between men and women in the mortal world. One might trip and fall into a betrothal or a scandal so easily, no matter whether one had the least bit of romantic interest in the gentleman in questions (or gentlemen at all!).

She escorted Dash away without looking back.

Ridiculous, to get caught up in an intimate conversation today of all days. She did not need friends, acquaintances — or worst of all, gentlemen suitors. She needed to keep her wits about her, and after tonight...

After tonight, Flavia Wednesday would no longer exist. Her charade would be over.

~

His conversation with Miss Wednesday was the highlight of Rinaldo's day. For a brief moment, conversing with an intelligent stranger, his spirits lifted a little.

He had been on edge since breakfast. As the afternoon grew long, and the merry bustle of the fair continued, Rinaldo found the old dread settling deep in his stomach. Crime was not something he could ever contemplate in comfort. As far back as the orphanage, even the thought of breaking a rule (no matter how unjust that rule) made him ill and panicky.

His brother had no such qualms. That was what had got them into this trouble in the first place.

"Is it time yet?" Rinaldo asked in a low voice.

Orlando clapped his hands to make the Extraordinary Automaton (once more wearing their only top hat) dance in a jerky fashion for the latest crop of children and villagers. As the machine spun around in awkward circles, Orlando drew a small notebook from the pocket of his jacket, flipping it open in businesslike fashion. "I spotted Mr Graves the butler over by the cider tent, pretending he was not trying to catch out the housekeeper, Mrs Holloway, at her tipple. Meanwhile the cook, Mrs Dawes, is quite openly on her third glass at the beer tent. Three maids and two footmen accounted for, and the family Gloucester themselves are due to present the best vegetable ribbons in the pavilion upon the hour. All present and correct." He grinned, and tipped a wink at his brother. "There's the governess, of course, last seen sharing tea with the children in the cake tent. Did you want to check upon Mis Wednesday's position yourself?"

Rinaldo refused to be teased. A pretty girl one way or another made no difference to him, with the mission (the *crime*) at hand. Or, come to that, under *any* circumstances, but he could never convince his brother that was true. "What of the gardener and his boy?"

"They don't sleep in at the big house, and they have the half day off like everyone else." Orlando gave him a scornful look. "I do check these things."

It was true. Rinaldo's brother, in many respects a lazy good-for-nothing of the highest order, was meticulous when plotting out schemes.

"We'd better get on our way," said Rinaldo, not wanting to sound reluctant. The time to voice his

concerns about this particular mission (*crime*) was long
past and besides, they had little choice in the matter.

The most dangerous enchantress in London had
their balls in a vice. If turning to criminal activity was
what it took to save them (at least, to save Orlando)
from the disaster that their life had become, then it was
worth it. Wasn't it?

Orlando clapped out a rhythmic pattern. The
onlookers cheered and laughed as the Extraordinary
Automaton yawned and stretched, then laid himself
down on the grass and produced a most noisome snore.
Now Rinaldo could see why his brother had insisted
on placing soap in the creature's innards: every
grumble and hiccup produced frothy bubbles from the
mouth that thoroughly delighted the smaller members
of their audience.

"Clever touch," Rinaldo noted. Orlando's loss of
magic had, if nothing else, made him more creative.

"Thanking you, Professor," said his brother with a
bow of self-mockery.

While the Extraordinary Automaton continued to
draw the attention of the crowd, the Extraordinary and
Miraculous Device Brothers set out to steal the only
thing worth stealing from the big house on the hill...

The gateway to another world.

~

"Ｎo interest in the governess, then?" Orlando huffed as they made their way up the hill.

Rinaldo rolled his eyes at him. "Don't tell me *you're* interested. That means she's bound to have a dark secret, and we'll end up kidnapped and cursed." They were still paying for Orlando's last romantic folly... and the one before that.

"I didn't say I was interested," his brother drawled. "She's far too smart and sensible for my tastes. I thought perhaps you —"

"Well, I don't," Rinaldo said abruptly. He thought they had gotten past these conversations years ago, but here Orlando was, testing him again. As if it was unthinkable they might differ in this one respect, when they were different in countless other ways. "You know I don't," he added, with a little less heat.

"I thought perhaps," said Orlando. "If you met the right lady."

Rinaldo almost stopped walking. "This again?"

"You might forget about —"

"I'm not nursing a lovelorn secret, or a broken heart. I just don't. Can we never discuss this again?"

They continued up the hill.

"It wouldn't have to be a lady, you know," Orlando said in a quiet mutter. "I wouldn't judge."

Rinaldo whirled on his brother. "You wouldn't judge. You, king of poor decisions in the bedchamber, would not judge me for having a man as a sweetheart, something which is a *hanging offence* in this country? How generous of you."

Orlando looked startled. "I only meant —"

"We are literally in this mess because you can't keep your dick to yourself," Rinaldo said between gritted teeth. "Be grateful that mine has no interest in anyone, or we could be in twice the peril on a daily basis."

"That's fair," Orlando agreed reluctantly.

"So glad you think so."

"But if you ever do, you have my support. You know. With your dick."

Rinaldo punched his brother lightly on the shoulder. "Glad to know that my pure and abiding lust for the science of miracles meets with your approval."

They were nearly at the top now, and Rinaldo thought at last, finally, they might be able to turn their attention to the job (*crime*) at hand.

"Did you bring this up to distract me so I wouldn't be nervous about what we're about to do?" he blurted out suddenly.

Orlando winked at him. "Would I do such a thing, brother mine?"

~

"**S**o this is Gloucester Worth," said Rinaldo as they let themselves in through the front gate and strolled up the path. No one was supposed to be home, and yet he found himself surveying the area anxiously. Their boots crunched loudly on the decorative pebbles.

They were dressed in their makeshift costumes from the fair: their flame-proof coats were the best thing they had to wear during metallurmagic demonstrations, and dark enough to conceal them as night came on. One hundred and one uses. Thank goodness they had rescued these garments, at least, when the witch took everything else.

"A mighty seat," said Orlando, as if quoting something out of a book. "The hearth and home of the Gloucester family, saviours of the world and defenders of free will."

"Merchants and misers," replied Rinaldo, who was not feeling especially heroic, and wanted to take it out on someone. "No magical wards on the front gate," he noted.

"Scuttlebutt says that it's not just Lady Carolinge who has it in for magic," said Orlando, as if Rinaldo had not actually been present while his brother flirted with a succession of Susans over the last week, picking up details about their employers. "Lord Salisbury refuses to bring magicians into the house, or use even the most everyday spells, except for travel to the

London house. Puritans or Good Queen Bess-ites, I suppose – they swallow everything the priests tell them about how using a cough philtre or an anti-fever posset will bring the fairies back and turn the world to dung."

"You don't generally find anti-magic zealots in a house that owes its fortune to philtres," said Rinaldo, his eyes darting back and forth as they walked up the main drive. Waltzing in as if they owned the place was all very well, as long as they didn't get caught. "Not to mention, a house guarding a gateway to you-know-where."

"If the toffs can't afford to be hypocrites, who can?"

"Garden?"

"Garden."

They circled around the mighty manor. It loomed over them with oppressive majesty. That odd feeling that the house was glaring at them was not a trick of the fading light at all, Rinaldo decided. Gloucester Worth disliked them deeply. He hadn't felt such architectural animosity since he first crossed the threshold of Number 12, Actaeon Place, back in London. Luckily the Device brothers didn't need to set foot inside this particular manor.

On the far side of Gloucester Worth, the garden stretched out in a confection of greenery. Rinaldo saw trees shaped like exotic animals, flowers like pompoms, and the truly sinister mouth of what had to be a maze. Nothing like a door into a magical forest, though. "It's not here."

"Patience, Professor," teased his brother. "Our patron isn't likely to have got the intelligence wrong, not when it comes to the Gloucesters and their treasures. It should be gaping open, if our girl has done her work. Let's investigate further."

Patron. That sounded almost respectable considering that the enchantress Lady Mortmain had blackmailed and threatened them both into being here – not to mention dosing Orlando with yet another of those love philtres of which she was so fond.

A shadow fell over them both, long and deep. Rinaldo whipped his head around and stared. "The Gloucesters don't approve of magic, you said."

"Indeed I did," said his brother, prodding at the opening to the maze as if it might hold the secrets they were searching for.

"So they wouldn't have magical protections on their garden?"

"Why do you ask?"

"*Run!*"

"Wha —" Orlando only half turned around, and barely had a chance to see the danger for himself. Rinaldo shoved his brother hard to start him off and then overtook him, streaking ahead as they ran.

Behind them, an enormous hedgerow in the shape of a dragon pursued them on four lumbering legs, trailing roots and dirt with every stomp.

TOUCHSTONE:
   Ay, now am I in Arden; the more fool I;
when I was
   at home, I was in a better place; but
travellers must be content.

— William Shakespeare, *As You Like It*,
Act II, Scene IV

Chapter 6

In Which Fountains Are Lost and Found

It was 6 o'clock: a good time for high tea, if nursery tea had not been previously enjoyed (though Flavia was certain that three toffee apples and four jam scones at the fair for young Dashmond counted as both nursery and high tea put together, regardless of a lack of sardines).

Dash was tired. He trailed along the path from the village, dragging at Flavia's hand and whining about having to leave the fair. Queenie, on the other hand, was thoroughly bored of the festivities, and keen to return to the house so she could check on her more recent experiments. Attempting to make both children walk at a similar pace was a challenge for Flavia, especially as she had to keep her own temper at the same time.

The closer they got to Gloucester Worth, the sicker she felt in the pit of her stomach. "No, wait," she said to the children. "We're not going in yet." If she allowed them to return to the nursery even for a short while, she would never get up the courage to do what must be done tonight.

"Why not?" Queenie demanded.

"Hurrah, are we going back to the fair?" Dash asked at the same time.

"I require you to each take a drop of cod liver oil before we go inside," said Flavia, drawing the small vial from her chatelaine. She had used the oil on them many times, let them see where she kept the bottle, and made it a thoroughly normal routine.

The house glared at her, daring her to do anything of which it disapproved. But cod liver oil was part of a governess's essential duties, and the house could do nothing to gainsay her.

"Yuck," said Dash, clamping his mouth shut.

"Out here?" said Queenie. "How rustic. Mother would be horrified."

"Yes," said Flavia, knowing a weapon when she saw one. "She would, wouldn't she?"

As simple as that, Queenie took the dose without blinking. Flavia turned her attention to Dash. "I bought a liquorice wheel at the fair," she told him. "You can have it if you take this drop right now, for your poor belly."

"A whole one?" said Dash, eyes wide. His mouth opened at the thought of an entire liquorice wheel all to himself.

"Oh yes," said Flavia, and dosed him as well. "Now, children, do you hear me?"

"We do," they replied. Apart from a glazed look about their eyes, they both appeared perfectly normal.

"You will be good and do everything I say, won't you?" she said, keeping her voice low and assured, as she had been taught. Nothing to see here but a governess and the children in her charge.

"Yes, Miss Wednesday," the children chorused. That was the only sign that there was something terribly wrong. Queenie and Dash had never acted in unison their entire lives.

"Come along into the garden," Flavia told them.

She would have to forgive herself, afterwards. That was all there was to it. No one else would do it for her.

This part would not hurt them.

She led the children, unreasonably docile, to the spot she had been eying from the corner of the garden. An ornamental archway; quite ordinary, leading nowhere in particular. But it hummed, as they approached.

"Recognise them," she whispered, pushing Dash and Queenie through the arch before she could change her mind. "Know them."

The blood of the Gloucester family was the key, and their presence unlocked it. The arch shimmered before Flavia, becoming something else... a heavier shape, a more solid archway, leading into a place that once bled magic into this world on a daily basis.

The Gate Sinister opened, to let them through.

From his hiding place in a thicket of hawthorn bushes thick with white May blossom, Rinaldo Device heard rustling in the leaves. He longed to know if it was Orlando, but did not dare to speak in case he drew the beast's attention to his hiding place.

There was something perverse about hiding from a rampaging hedge inside another hedge. He wished he had not thought that. Could hedges communicate with each other? Did they speak the same language?

"Psst," said his brother.

"Shush," Rinaldo whispered back, relieved that Orlando had not yet gotten his fool head bitten off. "Stay hidden."

"I'm not hidden," his brother said aloud. "I'm standing here, minding my own business. And I can see your shoes, Professor. You're not doing a fair job of hiding, either."

Rinaldo climbed out of the bush, picking sharp twigs out of his collar. "Any sign of that dragon?"

"Must have got bored and wandered off." Somehow Orlando had fallen in mud, though there was none nearby. It was a talent he had. His shirt was quite ruined, and his waistcoat would need repair as well as careful cleaning.

"Should I be insulted?" asked Rinaldo. "Were we not interesting prey? Didn't offer a tasty supper?" He felt a wet spot on his coat and cursed as he came up with a pocket of broken glass. The vial with their last supply of the Love-Me-Not philtre had cracked when he threw himself to the ground. "Damn it all."

"Can't say why it stopped chasing us," said Orlando, craning his neck back through the trees. "It pulled up in a hurry after we ducked through that archway."

"Which archway?"

"Made of stone, half hidden in the roses. I can't see it now. Funny..."

Slowly, Orlando and Rinaldo turned their heads to stare at each other.

"Does this garden smell different to you?" Rinaldo asked.

"Muddy?" said his brother. "And also, grassy?"

"I mean — it smells new." Rinaldo looked properly at the bush he had been hiding behind, bright with white hawthorn blossoms. He was an idiot not to have spotted it before. The May was maying, though it was near the end of October. "Spring. It's *spring* here."

"We found it," said Orlando in a yelp of joy. "We got in! We've found the Forest of Arden! Hats off, gentlemen, you've earned a cup of ale."

It looked like any other forest. Rinaldo could not deny that there was something peculiar about it, to be so alive with spring flowers at this time of year. What were the odds that a family would have more than one secret magical forest concealed on their estate? This must be it.

He had expected more, though. This was a scrubby sort of place. Where were the majestic vistas and the sparkling magical fountains? Where was the sizzling atmosphere of fairy knights and eternal chivalry?

"It was supposed to be difficult," Rinaldo said, keeping his voice low. He could not help but be suspicious. "We brought the curse-breaking idols and the skeleton keys and the sparks kit." The pockets of his flame-proof coat fair clanked with all the equipment they had put together for this night's work. "How did we get in without using any of it?"

"We're destined to be here," said Orlando. "The Forest of Arden invited us in. She wants us to be here." He whooped at the trees, leaping unexpectedly at one and throwing his mucky self up into the branches like a trained monkey.

No, not that, thought Rinaldo as his brother horsed around. *Someone came in here ahead of us, and opened the way.*

How many different schemes were entangled here tonight?

∼

For Flavia, the Forest of Arden smelled like home. It was a dreamy contrast to Gloucester Worth, with its heavy stone walls and harsh charms that prevented her from even dreaming of her true family. Once she stepped through the hidden gateway and into Arden, she finally let all those tensions fall away, and it was glorious.

The only place that Flavia had ever felt truly at home, outside her dreams of Faerie, was in the garden of Great-Aunt Primula Millicent's cottage – not Surrey, as she had told Lady Carolinge, but here in Kent, as far from the village of Shuttlesworthing as Primula Millicent Wednesday could bear to go without leaving the county altogether. Flavia had adored that tiny postage stamp of a garden, with its foxgloves and sweet peas and ornamental borders filled with pansies and heartsease.

The Forest of Arden felt more real than the cottage garden ever had. Flavia inhaled the heady scent of power and magic and so much tree that she would never run out of air.

The forest sang to Flavia in a steady, yearning voice: *Laurel-beech-birch-yew-fir-ash-olive-elm-oak-laurel-beech-birch-yew-fir-ash-olive-elm-oak-laurel-beech...*

No wonder her true mother craved it so badly, this forest that once was the playground of fairies and humans alike, standing empty all these centuries since the decree of Good Queen Bess.

Mostly empty. There had been one visitor in all that time that Flavia knew about: the thief who stole the heart of the Forest of Arden, and made his fortune from the spoils. Richard Gloucester.

The colours here were paler than those of the dream trees she had imagined since she first learned of her mission. The air tasted of spring promise but it was also slightly stale, as if it had been spring for a very long time, and summer still an eternity away.

The Forest of Arden might be a shadow of its former glory, but Flavia was going to change all that. Her sacrifice would be worthy.

The children walked with slow, heavy footsteps along the chamomile path. The philtre in the dose of cod liver oil was designed to make them believe this was an ordinary evening, full of reading and games and bedtime routine.

She had mixed it from Queenie's own ingredients in the schoolroom after the children were in bed, two nights ago.

Now, Queenie and Dash mumbled familiar words and phrases beneath their breath, acting out a bedtime squabble without passion or conviction. Flavia kept her chin high, not letting her voice tremble whenever she spoke to them. "Queenie, put on your night-rail. Dash, wash your face and behind your ears. Every night, not only when you've been climbing sooty chimneys."

Don't be a ninny, Wednesday, she told herself sternly. Those words always took her back to the School of Good Wives and God's Mercy, where the mistresses drummed important lessons into every generation of future governesses and nursemaids.

Miss Troughton of the Upper School was a sturdy games mistress who scorned ninnies and regularly encouraged the girls to buck up, have gumption, and above all, to 'rise above.' She was never specific about what travails were to be risen above but Flavia had only worked in domestic service for two days before she got the general idea.

You could rise above anything, if you had enough gumption. Ninnies need not apply.

There was a power in a woman like Miss Troughton, who marched up and down their draughty school corridors like a sergeant in the army, snapping at the 'gels' until they learned not to cry, or feel sorry for themselves.

Whenever Flavia felt the need for confidence, she imagined herself as Miss Troughton, never married, tough as nails, swinging her arms when she marched into a room.

"Don't be sentimental about the children, whatever you do," she rapped out at them, on many an occasion. "Your job is not to love your charges, nor to give them the attention their parents withhold. *Your job is to make them better people.* Let them go into the world, strong and capable, forgetting that you ever existed."

The chamomile path was long. Flavia kept them marching along at a fair lick. She could not risk the children's absence being noticed, or one of the family following them into the Forest while the gate was open. She did not believe that the Gloucesters had eschewed magic altogether, no matter Lady Carolinge's distaste for the subject. Lord Salisbury and his brother knew that their job was to guard the garden. Perhaps they had taken that duty further, like their grandfather...

"One more story," muttered Dash beneath his breath, his hand reaching out to her. "Please, Miss Wednesday."

Flavia sighed, and took his hand. No sentiment. No love. *Don't be a ninny, Wednesday.*

Still, it was for the best that the children did not trip and fall. A little hand-holding would do no harm. "Very well," she said as if it was just another bedtime in the nursery. "One more story. But it's your last, Master Dashmond."

Show some gumption.

Heroic deeds required sacrifice. Every fairy tale told you that.

~

"Here we are," said Rinaldo. He and Orlando had explored the Forest of Arden for what felt like hours. The wretched place did not compare favourably to the version they had read about in stories. There was a singular lack of magical fountains or seductive enchantresses, not to mention nymphs, knights or other stock characters from *Bulfinch's Mythology*. He was beginning to suspect that their quest was ill founded. Also, Lady Mortmain should have provided them with a map.

The forest felt warm and familiar, a good place to be. Rinaldo didn't trust that feeling at all. Spells that messed with your head were bad. Worst of all were the spells that made you feel like there was nothing to worry about. He knew where he was with metal and magic, but anything to do with thoughts and feelings gave him the shivers.

For all its scrubby plants and thin, spindly trees over-laden with blossom, the Forest of Arden felt… joyous. Delight washed through the trees like dappled sunlight, as if the Forest was glad to have people walking through it again, even if they were not the heroes of chivalric myth. And never would be, if Rinaldo had a say in the matter.

"Getting anything from that bauble?" he growled.

Orlando reached into his shirt and pulled out the witch's ruby that hung on a chain around his neck. "It's not saying hot or cold, or anything useful in the way of direction. For an enchanted jewel, it's remarkably lacking in conversation."

"Some sign that this isn't a trap would be ideal," said Rinaldo.

"See, it's written right here on the gem, Not A Trap," Orlando teased, then punched Rinaldo lightly in the arm when he didn't fall for it. "Can't promise miracles, Professor." He gave the gem a thoughtful tap and let it hang out of his shirt instead of hiding it away again. "You're the one who makes the plans. Which direction should we go?"

Rinaldo resisted the urge to suggest they should consult a copy of Shakespeare's *As You Like It*. They had not thought to bring one with them. "Given that neither of us are blessed with divination skills, I suggest we keep going until we find those enchanted fountains everyone writes about."

"And not drink from any of them," said Orlando, nodding his head seriously.

Rinaldo clipped his brother about the head with the side of his hand.

"I said *not* drink from them!" Orlando protested, ducking away.

"Sensible fellows wouldn't have to make that promise."

His brother puffed out his chest. "I've never been sensible."

Sadly, this was more than true. "We've no antidote left. Not even a drop, unless you want to lick the broken glass in my pocket. Keep your mouth to yourself."

"Got it." Orlando smiled hopefully. "You don't have to worry about me."

Too late for that. Rinaldo had spent most of his life worrying about his brother. He wasn't going to stop now they had landed themselves in the middle of a magical forest that was being too nice to them, while probably wanting them dead.

Orlando crowed suddenly and darted off into the trees as if he had spotted a clue. Rinaldo chased him until he came upon a bright marble fountain in a clearing of trees. Orlando stood gazing upon the sculpted façade with something close to adoration. "What do you think? Fountain of Youth, Fountain of Love-Me-Not?"

To Rinaldo's horror, his brother leapt up upon the edge of the marble edifice, leaning perilously close to the water that bubbled up from within.

"Fountain of Nightmares, Fountain of Blindness, Fountain of Death," Rinaldo said pointedly, wanting to physically grab Orlando and throw him over his shoulder. He would knock him *unconscious* if he had to.

Orlando laughed. "Always look on the bleak side, don't you, Professor? Don't worry your pretty little head, I know we have a job to do." He shifted his feet, practically straddling the fountain. Playing the stage magician, he reached into one of the voluminous pockets of his flame-proof coat and produced a small, gleaming item.

The clockwork beetles were one of their proudest inventions, back when they were in Her Majesty's good books. Rinaldo felt a momentary pang.

See how far we have fallen, brother?

No time for self-pity now. He must be prepared for whatever had to be done. They would never get their lives back if they did not follow Lady Mortmain's instructions to the letter.

"Now's the time to change our mind," Orlando said, dangling the clockwork beetle by a single brass mandible. "You're sure?" He relied on Rinaldo to be his conscience.

Rinaldo swallowed down his guilt. Doing the right thing was not the priority, not tonight. Saving Orlando was the only thing that mattered. "Do you want to stay in thrall to an enchantress, doing nothing but her bidding to the end of time?" Rinaldo demanded, pushing down his own concerns.

Orlando hesitated. "That does seem like my inevitable destiny. Based on past experience."

"Sod destiny," said Rinaldo. "Steal the damned potion so we can get out of here."

Orlando opened his hand, letting the clockwork beetle fall into the water of the fountain. After a moment there was a skittering sound as the thing clambered back up the side of the well.

Orlando shook the excess liquid off the beetle carefully, and checked that its belly was full before popping it back in a pocket. So much safer than carrying a pocket full of glass vials, as Rinaldo and tonight's little accident could attest.

"One fountain down," said Orlando brightly. "How many to go?"

"Twelve," said Rinaldo. "According to legend, and Lady Mortmain."

"So, we have a long night ahead of us." With a wicked grin, and only a little sleight of hand, Orlando produced a second beetle. "Might as well work for ourselves as well as the She-beast of Number 12." He dropped the new beetle in the fountain, and cupped an ear to listen to it fall.

Rinaldo's heart sank. "You fancy risking the wrath of the most dangerous enchantress in London to score a spare measure of philtre when we don't even know which it is? She made you swear *blind* you would only take samples for her, not skite off with extras."

"I don't see why we shouldn't profit!" Orlando seized the second beetle when it made its way back to him, and tucked it into a different pocket, before leaping athletically to the ground. "After all, I'm the one with the most to lose."

"Don't I know it," said Rinaldo with a heavy heart.

I t had been dusk for hours: never properly growing light or dark. Flavia was disoriented, and the smell of magical blossom made her nose itch. The Forest of Arden sang to her constantly, wanting her to play and dance and enjoy its company. Part of her wanted to give up on her mission, to throw herself into the trees and roll around in the grass forever with no more cares about children or fairies or true mothers or sacrifices, but she had a job to do.

Flavia's feet were heavy on the path. Queenie and Dash were exhausted, stumbling in their stupor. Finally she made them lie down on the soft springy ground to rest. There were so many paths in this forest, seen and unseen. There was no reason to think that anyone following them (should anyone of the Gloucester family even think to follow them) would choose this particular path, and the herbal aroma was sure to disguise their scent from being tracked.

"Sleep," she whispered, passing her hands over each of their faces, allowing a little of her natural magic to escape. Dash and Queenie fell like stones into a deep slumber, lying still as if dead.

Flavia sat with her back against a stately elm and hugged her knees as she waited out the endless, eternal dusk of the Forest of Arden. Finally the sky darkened and a silver moon slid overhead.

Don't be a ninny, Wednesday.

She did not sleep.

There is no position in the household subject to greater moral responsibility than that of the resident governess. In selecting the person who shall have total and complete influence over the growing children of the family, it is important to ensure that their mode of thought, their model of behaviour and even their philosophies on such polarising topics as the function of magic in common purpose, or the ethical conundrum of love philtres in modern marriages, be as close as possible to the mother and father's own wishes and desires.

— Mrs Morrigan's Guide to Household
Etiquette (1832)

Chapter 7

In Which Enchantments Leave a Bitter Aftertaste

Rinaldo lost Orlando to the Forest of Arden only once, when a bright green butterfly distracted his brother off the path and led him into a patch of bracken that smelled of sleeping spells. Rinaldo hauled him out in the nick of time, and now they were both drowsy and irritable, but still on their feet. It was a blooming miracle.

Five fountains down now, seven to go.

They had water to drink, thanks to a flask Rinaldo had stored in one of his many pockets, but he rationed their sips. He had presumed one flask would be sufficient for their night's work, now but he was starting to wonder. The Forest of Arden was broader and deeper than he had ever imagined.

There was little alive in this place, beyond the botanical. That single butterfly was the only creature they had seen stirring in the trees since the hedge dragon chased them in here in the first place. No birds. How could there be so many trees and yet no birds?

Rinaldo tripped over a root and skidded awkwardly down a dirt slope, closely followed by his brother, who laughed at him. Then Orlando broke off, staring into the distance. Rinaldo followed his gaze.

Ahead of them was a wide expanse of grass cut into dark and light squares, like a chessboard. Creatures lined up along the squares, each of them cut from hedge shapes as that dragon had been, back in the garden of Gloucester Worth. There were more dragons here, along with unicorns, centaurs and other chimaera.

"Are they going to come alive and chase us too?" asked Orlando, his voice too loud in this quiet place.

Rinaldo shushed him, but the creatures slept on, or else were not alive.

"There's a fountain," Orlando whispered.

It felt as if they were being watched, if not by the enormous topiary creatures, then by something else hidden in the bushes. "Quickly and quietly," Rinaldo urged.

They crept across the chessboard to the fountain on the far side. This particular fountain was built from a dark granite, and made no noise as water dribbled slowly over a series of stone spheres. If Rinaldo was a betting gentleman, he would mark this one out as the Fountain of Death.

One of the topiary unicorns twitched. "Let's move

on to somewhere we're less likely to be stabbed by the shrubbery," he suggested.

For once, Orlando did not argue. He dropped two the clockwork beetles into the depths of the dark fountain, and rocked back on his heels. "Might as well collect the full set."

"Don't get any on your skin," Rinaldo warned.

"Teach your grandmother to suck eggs, Professor."

Even when the children woke, the enchantment held. They believed themselves to be in the nursery, on a new day. Flavia had brought a flask of water with her and made them drink small sips, sweetened with honey. She had no food, but the children did not complain of empty bellies. They imagined that they ate their usual breakfast, made stilted conversation with their mother, and returned to the schoolroom.

She was the worst person in the world.

They walked again, the children shuffling in their hallucinatory world and Flavia stepping along beside them. She had not considered what it would feel like, how slow and agonising this particular part of her mission would be.

Every step was heavy. It was a struggle to lift her chin and walk with purpose, as Miss Troughton had taught her.

Finally the tangled trees thinned out ahead of her and Flavia saw a brighter kind of sunlight, fierce after so long in the shade. The chamomile path ahead of them ran directly into a glade of weeping willows exploding with silver-grey blossom and beyond that, the lake.

The Lake of All Worlds, her mother had whispered in her dreams for years, long before Flavia came to Gloucester Worth. *Only from within the secret forest can you open the path for us, the way of ways, and let us back into the world of men. The Forest of Arden will be ours again, and the Gloucester family will be punished for their years of theft and betrayal.*

First, the Forest of Arden would burst into new life and new magic, reconnected to the world of Faerie. Then, through the Gate Sinister that led to the garden of the Gloucester family, the fairies would stream out into the mortal world, and reclaim everything they had lost.

Humans would be their meat and drink again. Their loves, their pets, their entertainment.

All the ways between worlds would be open. Flavia need never be separate from her true mother again. She could return home any time she liked; she could stay forever in Faerie and never set foot into the human world again. This was the task she had been born for. It was supposed to be easy.

Easy as dancing.

"Walk a little slower, Queenie," she whispered, her

eyes fixed on the weeping willows and the shining waters of the lake. The girl obeyed her.

"Can I work in the laboratory all day today, Miss Wednesday?" she asked, her voice clear as day. "I must work harder. I'm running out of time."

"You work so hard," said Flavia. "A holiday will do you no harm."

"Oh no, Miss Wednesday," said Queenie, sounding shocked. "I lost a whole day to the village fair. I must work now." Her throat had a rasp to it. Were the children thirsty?

Flavia stopped them both and brought her water flask to their lips, pretending it was cocoa, a special treat with elevenses. They sipped obediently, and smacked their lips with pleasure.

She had not allowed her skin to turn its natural green yet, here in the Forest of Arden. There was no reason why she should hold back. Children who believed they were drinking cocoa in the nursery rather than the last drops of flask water in a long lost magical forest were not going to turn a hair because of the colour of their governess.

But after so many weeks — months — *years* pretending to be something she was not among the mortals, Flavia could not bear to let the illusion fall too soon. She was not ready.

"Tell me of your work, Queenie," she said in her brisk governess voice, because anything was better than making them walk again. The lake was dangerously near. "Talk to me about something important."

"She's trying to make the best stink bomb in the world," said Dash, and laughed so hard he snorted.

"I'm going to restore our family fortune," said Queenie with confidence. She had said that before, but Flavia had never questioned her in more detail.

A sound jarred Flavia away from those thoughts. Were those men's voices? She drew the children quickly into the nearest scrubby bushes, thick with flowers that made the air sweet. More like cakes than flowers. "Hush now," she insisted, but the children did not obey as quickly this time. Was the enchantment wearing off? She did not want to dose them again, but dare not risk them coming awake before she had done what she must.

"Great-grandfather made his fortune selling philtres," Dash informed her.

"Yes, I know about that." Flavia was well versed in the history of the Gloucesters, and the late Richard Gloucester, first Earl of Shuttlesworth, in particular. "He was famous. Shhh now, darlings. Only a little longer."

"He died without sharing his most famous formula," Queenie went on stubbornly, her voice rising. "If I can figure it out, I won't have to marry for money like father did. I can be free."

Flavia was so close to putting a hand over the girl's mouth to keep her quiet, but she hesitated at that. "All

girls have to marry," she said finally. "Don't be wet."
Miss Troughton had never married. Miss Troughton
had sailed through the world like a military barge,
shoulders back, chin up, training an army of 'gels with
gumption' to conquer Britannia, one household at a
time.

*A governess rules her schoolroom with a firm hand,
and stands for no nonsense.*

"Rich ones don't," said Queenie loftily, getting
some of the pink back in her cheeks. Oh yes, the
enchantment was wearing off. Flavia rummaged in her
chatelaine for the vial. "Rich heiresses can choose who
they marry, or choose not to marry at all. It won't only
mean my own freedom. If I discover Great-grandfather's antidote, no one will ever have to marry someone
they don't love."

Oh, the poor child. She thought that Richard
Gloucester had invented the Love-Me-Not philtre,
instead of stealing it from the Forest of Arden all those
years ago. She had been trying to recreate it with
alchemy. Flavia was glad for a moment that Queenie
would never know how impossible her task had been.

Dash leaned against the nearest tree, looking
sleepy. "Mother loves us really," he said in a quiet
mutter.

"No," Queenie said in a soft breath. "She doesn't.
She tries, Miss Wednesday, she really does. But the
philtre makes her love Father best. She'd be free of
him, if I had grandfather's antidote."

The philtre makes her love Father best. Flavia had suspected as much. "Your father gave your mother a love philtre."

Queenie nodded slackly. "On her wedding day. She agreed to it, and he was going to take one too, but his people didn't like the idea, so he let her take it alone. Wouldn't it be awful to be under a spell, not to be able to make choices for yourself? Great-grandfather's formula changed the world, so no one ever had to be enchanted against their will, but now it's lost. We can't make more, and Britannia is running out, one drop at a time."

"You're going to save the world from love philtres?" Flavia asked.

"Yes," said Queenie, lifting her chin. In that instant, so sure of her resolve, she looked a lot like Miss Troughton.

Flavia's hand closed too tightly around the vial. "You're very clever," she said finally. "I'm sure you can do it."

"Of course I can," Queenie said scornfully, and then blinked and looked around. She gave a little scream. "Miss Wednesday, where are we?"

Flavia pressed the vial on her, splashing another drop on her lower lip. Queenie's eyes glazed over instantly.

"I'm sorry," Flavia said, and it came out as a sob.

Wouldn't it be awful to be under a spell, not to be able to make choices for yourself?

All girls have to marry. Don't be wet.

Sentiment has no place in a school room. Your job is not to love these children.

"I don't have a choice," Flavia whispered, hugging both children close. If only she had not come to enjoy their company. This would be so much easier if they were horrid, spoiled little beasts. It would be easy as dancing. Easy as smashing an egg into a bowl.

Dash was all but asleep. When Flavia let go of him, he crumpled beneath the nearest tree. Queenie was very pale, her hands moving as if she continued to work with her glass tubes and recipes on the long laboratory bench. Endlessly working to save the world, in the hope she could prevent a fate that awaited all respectable young women of aristocratic households.

"I have a world to save," Flavia told them. Not that they cared. Why should they?

She was close enough now to hear her mother's voice in the rustle of the trees above her, in the breath of the forest, in the scent of spicy eucalypt and sour willow. *Give me the children. You can be yourself, at last. The fairies of Britannia will be free and you will be whole... we can be together.*

Flavia had been waiting for this night for years, ever since she first learned who she was and where she came from. Since she learned of her mission. All she had to do was hand these children over to the Queen, and she would have everything she ever wanted.

Cruellest thought of all: *Perhaps I don't have to sacrifice them both.*

That shocked her, like a burst of cold water to the face. Choose one to return home, and one to be sacrificed to the fairies. Wasn't that a reasonable compromise?

Dashmond was the heir to the family. His parents would choose him to live, if they had to. But Queenie, clever and bright, she was the one dedicated to saving her family's fortunes and changing the world.

Looking down at them both, still caught in the horrible fantasy of only sacrificing one, Flavia knew in her heart for the first time that she could not kill either of them.

At the School of Good Wives and God's Mercy, one was encouraged to speak like a respectable gentlewoman at all times. Never so much in all her life had Flavia wished she knew how to curse like a sailor.

Her mother was wrong to believe in her. Everything they had worked towards, everything Flavia had promised, every dream she had ever danced. She had to let it all go, if she was going to save Queenie and Dashmond. *She was so weak.*

Damn. Damn it all to hell.

Queenie's hands flicked back and forth, shifting her imaginary experiments in the air, in those glass bubbles of which she was so fond. "I will save the world for girls like me," she said with a little sigh.

"Yes," Flavia said. Her mind was made up, then.

"Yes, you will. That's all right, then," she added, mostly for her own benefit.

Time for a new plan.

Flavia got the children to their feet and urged them back up the chamomile path a little way before she shoved them off it, directly into the undergrowth. She had to half-carry Dash, who was no lightweight, especially with the bracken and twigs catching at her stockings as she hurried them along.

They're not coming after you, not yet, she chided herself, but could not slow her steps.

She turned here and there, determined to be unpredictable in the route she chose. Finally they burst through a thicket of trees, Flavia and the Gloucester children together, tumbling down a slope towards a pretty lawn that had remained perfect for hundreds of years. In the centre of the wide lawn was a massive topiary chess set, peopled with yew hedges cut into the shapes of animals rather than traditional chess pieces.

It was distressing to see plants treated like whimsical toys of humans. But Flavia had no moral ground to stand on, and it was as good a hiding place as any. She would be able to find her way back here, if she needed to, by listening for the song of the yew.

She lay Queenie down first, between a large topiary peacock and a sphinx. She stroked the girl's hair, and bid her to sleep deeply. Queenie's face relaxed as she surrendered to her governess with complete trust, and fell deep.

Dash next. Flavia lay him down beside his sister, so they could share a sort of warmth. "Dashmond," she said clearly in his ear, using the stern voice she saved for when there was a very important instruction to be conveyed. "If anyone finds you here, you must turn into a dragon and use your flame upon them. Especially if..." And she hesitated, but only for a moment. "Especially if that person is green. Do you understand?"

The boy nodded muzzily and began to snore. She patted him once, and then unfastened her over-dress and pulled over her head, using it to blanket the children. Things were likely to get messy, and if she survived the next few hours, she would need her dress to be clean and dry. She removed her stockings and boots as well, laying them in a tidy pile.

They would be safe here, for now. Safe even from Flavia, should that be necessary. She hoped that it would not.

Dressed only in her voluminous cambric petticoats, Flavia climbed up the slope again and marched through the enchanted forest, letting her sensitive nose guide her back to the chamomile path. She felt better than she had in weeks, as if a burden had finally lifted off her aching shoulders.

She had made her choice.

She would not betray the children.

She must instead summon the gumption to betray her mother.

Buck up, Wednesday. Don't be a ninny.

～

Orlando was twitchy. Rinaldo ignored this at first. They had completed their mission — every fountain in this wretched museum of enchanted trees had donated two samples of unknown magical philtre to their clockwork vials. Orlando's flame-proof coat was damp in places, but rattling with fat-bellied beetles, exactly half of which he intended to present to their patron, the enchantress Lady Mortmain.

They were free and clear, their crime complete. Now they must exit the stage and disappear into the too-damned-dark-to-see-anything night. Back to London and civilisation and the vile hag who sent them here in the first place.

But there was something wrong with Orlando. He startled at every snapped twig or fallen shadow. As they made their way through a tangled web of weeping willows, Rinaldo's brother tripped over his own boots, lurched forward with a muddy squelch and then stopped stock still. "Bollocks," he swore.

"What is it now?" Rinaldo demanded.

"Fairies," said Orlando, peering up into the weeping willow tree above him that did, admittedly, form a gnarled tangle, as if it had been copied from a book of tales to scare children. There were so many willows here, clustered together in a gruesome mess of fronds.

Trees had never seemed so sinister.

"It's not fairies," sighed Rinaldo. "It's never fairies. Why have we stopped?"

"This is the Forest of Arden, the infamous enchanted land that bested all manner of paladins by seducing them, tricking them and murdering them," Orlando said hotly. "How can you deny the possibility of fairies?"

"I don't deny the possibility of fairies!" Rinaldo snapped back. "But they were *banished*. Good Queen Bess made sure there wasn't a fairy left in Arden when she sacked the place. So I think you have to agree that the possibility of finding fairies here is very thin indeed. You're not losing your bottle, are you?" *Or your marbles.*

"My mother used to tell stories about fairies," said Orlando in a low voice.

Rinaldo stilled. His brother rarely spoke of the time before the orphanage. If it was an unwritten rule then it was one that Orlando himself had devised, knowing that Rinaldo had no family memories of his own to fall back on.

This was a good sign. Orlando speaking of something from the early years of his life – particularly a story Rinaldo had never heard before – that was *good*. It shouldn't shoot fear into Rinaldo's chest, or twist like a knife in his belly.

"What did she say?" Rinaldo asked finally.

Orlando stayed standing still, tangled in the tree fronds, his boots vanished into the muck. "Most people believe Britannian fairies are gone for good, but people always say such things about creatures they fear. She said she could taste magic in the air, and it was angry about what mortals had done to tame it." Orlando shrugged uncomfortably. "She said it as she was dying, so I always reckoned it was important. She also said that Britannian fairies smell of mint if they smell of anything and I've smelt nothing but peppermint for the last five bleeding minutes."

"What does that have to do with the philtres or the fountains?" Rinaldo asked, refusing to accept *peppermint* as a reason to get distracted. "We're done, we can go back to Lady Mortmain now and fix you, we can get on with our lives. We're *done*." He didn't want to hear Orlando telling stories about his mother.

Orlando nodded, pulling himself together. "You're right, Professor. We should get out of here. And — we should avoid the lake. All the stories say that Queen Bess exiled all of Faerie to an island in the middle of a lake, which makes it the most dangerous place around here."

"No trouble with that," Rinaldo assured. "We'll steer clear of the lake, if it makes you feel better."

"Yes," said Orlando in an odd voice. "Only the thing about the lake is. I reckon I'm standing in it."

Acorn had never seen such a splendid tree in his life. "Jiminy," he said. "Are those bath buns hanging from the branches?"

"Indeed they are," said Molly with a blink of her eyes. "Crumpets too, all buttery. And jam tarts, my favourite!"

The children realised to their delight that every branch held some new wonder for the tea table: honey jumbles, cherry cake, and lashings of hard-boiled eggs. They stripped the branches with great efficiency, laying out a picnic on the soft grass.

Finally, his fingers digging hard into the bark of the tree, Colin discovered a teapot still steaming hot, and a red and white checked tablecloth.

"What a splendid spread!" said Dinah, as they tucked in to their heart's content.

"Oh dear," said Acorn a little while later, licking butter from his fingers with a smacking noise. He looked uneasily over his shoulder at *the tree, with its bare branches and snapped twigs. Sap ran out of the hole in its trunk as if it were weeping tears of judgement. "I think the tree might be a trifle displeased."*

— *Acorn's Dear Little Tea Party* (1865),
written and illustrated by Primula
Millicent Wednesday.

Chapter 8

On The Proper Etiquette for Thwarting Fairies

For most of her life, Flavia had wondered what it would be like, to stand on the shore of the Lake of All Worlds. She had imagined a connection, an intense feeling of belonging, of *home*.

The dark lake was surrounded by weeping willows, dipping their long fronds into the lake as if they were tears that tumbled directly from the sky. Out there, across the water, her true mother waited for her. Flavia's exile was almost at an end.

Except, of course, it would never be over. Not now.

She had imagined that the island would be visible from the shore, but the lake was unexpectedly enormous. Also, there was an eerie mist that prevented her from seeing very far. Her people were out there, invisible.

They would never forgive her.

Flavia took a long, ragged breath and stepped into

the water, feeling the soft reeds caress her ankles as the cold soaked into her skin and weighed down her petticoats.

The lake heaved a sigh. "Flaxenseed," it purred. "What have you done, little acorn?"

She knew that voice. She had heard it the first time she dreamed of Faerie. It was not the voice of her mother, it was the voice of her friend, her favourite person, her first love. Flavia frowned. "Not you, Quicksilver. I must speak with the Queen."

The water shimmered around her, forming a body of a lithe young woman, her face masked with green ivy. Faerie wore masks at all times, which they called their true faces: elaborate constructions of leaves and petals and bark.

They had never let Flavia make a mask for herself in her dreams. Not until she completed the mission they had sent her into the mortal world to do. Not until she proved her worth.

Quicksilver stared at her as if she was a stranger, as if she was not the same person Flavia had carried in her heart since she was twelve years old. Quicksilver's true face had none of the merry gleam that Flavia remembered. Nevertheless, she was beautiful. Fairies were good at beautiful.

Flavia had not dreamed since she first came to stay in Gloucester Worth. It was an age since she had felt Quicksilver's hand brush against hers, or her mouth hot and teasing against her throat.

"I am the Hand and Voice of the Queen, Flax-enseed," Quicksilver said, oddly formal. "What you have to say to her, you must say first to me. We would not wish to upset her, would we?"

"This is not a matter for a go-between," Flavia said through gritted teeth. Did Quicksilver suspect her already? Why was she acting so strange?

The eyebrows of the ivy leaf shape of Quicksilver's true face quirked, taking on a superior expression. "You have lived outside Faerie so long, little acorn. But that is no excuse for defying the customs of your mother's court."

"I'm not defying the customs, I am defying *you* because you are being rude," Flavia snapped. "Let me speak to my mother, right now."

"Such manners," Quicksilver taunted. "Is this what they have taught you, the grubby mortals? Is this what you teach their children?" Her silver eyes danced at Flavia from behind the mask.

Panic shot through her whole body. *She knows. How does she know?*

"Mother!" Flavia screamed across the water. "Tanaquil Gloriana, Queen of Queens! Listen to your humble servant, your daughter!"

Quicksilver slapped her across the face. Her body was nearly transparent, and yet the blow stung sharply. "Oh, Flaxenseed," she sang in a terrible voice. "*What have you done?*"

The trees shivered around them, and a figure

formed in the hanging willow fronds. This fairy was a statuesque woman with leafy hair falling past her hips into the water. Her mask was braided from branches, and flecked with tiny spring buds. She was enchanting, and terrible. She was everything.

"Daughter," said the Queen of Faerie in a hard voice. "Daughter, where is my sacrifice?"

Flavia had caught glimpses of the Queen all of her life, even before the dreams began. She saw fragments of Tanaquil Gloriana in mirror reflections and bodies of water, in the ancient apple tree outside the orphanage and in the flower displays of the park where she used to walk during on weekends when she was at the School of Good Wives and God's Mercy. A handful of times, Flavia was allowed into her mother's presence during the dancing dreams: a remote but majestic figure presiding over the endless, gnawing, floating Isle of Faerie.

She had never felt her presence in such a tangible way. It was overwhelming. She felt as if she was going to burst out of her skin, quite literally, pieces of her scattering in all directions. Her head hurt so hard she could barely think.

Kneel, submit, surrender.

"Mother," Flavia said, summoning up the will to explain herself.

"You brought the children," thundered Tanaquil Gloriana, who had been Queen of the Faerie for a thousand years, before and after her creatures were exiled from Britannia by the mortal Good Queen Bess. "You have brought my sacrifices, so that we can return to the world of mortals and take it for our own." These were not questions.

"No," said Flavia, her heart breaking. "I have not."

The sky cracked above them, raindrops spattering into the lake. Water soaked into her petticoats. An eerie, warm wind blew around them, whipping at her hair. Flavia felt the air pressure change, drawing in tight like a thunderstorm corseting her body. "I have not," she said lifting her chin. "I cannot give them to you. I'm so sorry."

"YOU LIE!" shrieked the wind and the rain and the willows. Rage tore the sky open with noise.

Quicksilver lunged at Flavia, dragging her cruelly to her knees in the lake water. "Where are they?" she hissed directly into Flavia's ear, wet and cold against her skin.

How had Flavia ever thought they were friends?

"At home in their beds!" Flavia screamed, not at Quicksilver, but at her mother. It was a truth of sorts, and she hoped that she was still far enough away from Faerie that these two could not grasp hold of the image that rose up in her mind of the two children, sleeping among the topiary chess pieces.

It had seemed so easy, when Quicksilver first sang the plan to her, hands warm in hers as they danced through the greenwood in Flavia's dreams. The children were not Queenie and Dash then, but nameless mortals whose family had committed great crimes against the Faerie and the Forest both. If only Flavia had not grown weak for those children, she might have saved her mother, and her people.

Too late now.

"I flung you from our prison on a dandelion seed before you first opened your eyes! I used our last strength to give you freedom, daughter," thundered the Queen. "This is how you repay my loyalty?" Her willow fronds lashed around Flavia, binding her wrists and ankles, biting savagely into her waist and throat. "You wound me. I must wound you in return."

Cold, watery fingers tore at her hair, her skin, her soaked garments. Flavia did not struggle, did not make a sound, did not even argue. *She's not really here, it must be taking all her magic to reach this far, she can't set foot in the Forest of Arden, not without the sacrifice, I must endure, chin up, don't be wet, she can't hurt me...*

Flavia kept believing that her mother's strength and pain and anger could last no longer, until she was dragged deeper into the cold lake water. It sucked on her limbs.

"Long live the Queen!" mouthed Quicksilver, ever the devoted servant. Flavia felt her hot breath on her cheek. *Not here. Neither of them are really here.*

Quicksilver grasped Flavia's arm in both hands and broke it with a snap.

O rlando wasn't wrong.

The long fronds of the willow trees hung low over the water. It almost did not look like water at all but a wide, wet and green surface. In the dim light of the long evening of the Forest of Arden, it could easily be mistaken for muddy grass.

Once you were up to your calves in that water, however, it became horribly obvious that it was a lake.

Rinaldo tugged on his brother's arm, trying to lever his body out of the sucking mud. "Only you could fall into a lake in the middle of a magical forest."

"I did not fall, I stepped," corrected Orlando with great dignity.

"I'm not buying you another pair of boots!"

"Send the bill to the fairies."

Rinaldo lost his temper. "There are no fairies. The fairies are entirely in your head, which makes sense because there had to be something in there apart from sawdust and stuffed cotton! We have to get back to the enchantress you sold us out to, before she wrecks our lives even further. Imaginary fairies are *not our problem right now*!"

"Mother, *no*!" A scream cut through the air. They were not alone in the Forest of Arden.

The brothers went still for a moment, and then Rinaldo helped his brother yank his muddy feet more successfully out of the lake, leaving the boots behind. He grabbed them next, and the boots practically brought half the swamp with them. Rinaldo trod gently as they made their way around the edge of the willow-fringed lake. Orlando made a lot of squishy sounds, walking in his wet socked feet.

"There," whispered Rinaldo. The greyish light was brighter here, allowing them to see more in the way of colours and shapes among the trees.

It was not every day that you saw a young lady with a wild tangle of green hair wrestling with trees in a lake. She looked like a maiden out of heroic legend, except that her skin was the same shade of sage as her hair, and instead of gleaming armour, her sturdy figure was wrapped in sodden layers of petticoat.

The girl struggled as the fronds of a wet weeping willow dragged her under the water, lashing her with spindly branches. The grey water rose up around her, alive with tiny lights, hissing and spitting at her face. Her right arm hung limp at her side. The lake and the trees were getting the better of her.

"Fairies," Orlando said in a triumphant whisper. "Didn't I tell you?"

Rinaldo could not deny it. "How was I to know you would be right about something? It happens so rarely. We shouldn't get involved," he whispered back.

"I'm not stupid, Professor." But this was Orlando, who intervened in every angry marital dispute or romantic duel he came across, a man who offered himself on a plate if there was a damsel or a crone to be defended. He could not help himself.

Rinaldo edged closer to his brother, ready to grab his sleeve if necessary. The last thing they needed was to get in the middle of a fairy feud, especially with the evidence of the crimes they had committed against this forest still tucked away in Orlando's coat pockets.

A face loomed up out of the tree branches, dark and angry, virulently green. *"Child, you have ruined everything!"* it screamed at the green girl in the petticoat — Miss Wednesday, surely it was Miss Wednesday, though she was rather less green of skin when Rinaldo last spoke with her.

"Mother, I'm sorry," wept the damsel. Blood. Was that blood down her white dress? Why was the blood also green?

"I made you and I can break you to pieces," howled the tree face.

"Hold there!" interrupted a horribly familiar voice.

Rinaldo looked around and saw that his brother was gone. Swearing, he scrambled to his own feet and dove through the trees after Orlando.

Who was running to the rescue. Of course.

❧

Flavia had known that her mother would be angry at her. She understood that she would suffer for her choice. She had not banked upon the sheer weight of the fury of Tanaquil Gloriana, Queen of Faerie. The tendrils of the weeping willow lashed at Flavia's skin.

Every time she fought back, Quicksilver turned the water against her, too. Caught between angry lake and furious tree, every time Flavia raised her head towards air and sky, she was dragged down deeper.

Pain burned down one side of her, drowning out all else. She bled green from countless cuts and scrapes.

This was the first time Flavia had ever denied her mother anything. Tonight was supposed to be the beginning of her new life as the fairy she was supposed to have been, instead of the outsider child who only glimpsed their revels in her dreams and never quite managed to perfect the steps of their dance.

Now she had no hope, no home. Nothing but the breath in her lungs, and she was damned if she was going to lose that too.

"You can hurt me all you want," Flavia yelled into the depths. "I won't give you the children. They're real people, not tools of vengeance. They deserve their freedom as much as you do!"

"You have no idea what vengeance looks like," declared the Queen of Faerie. The Forest of Arden shook with her anger.

If Flavia sacrificed the children to the lake, their blood would open the ways between worlds. It would allow Faerie to take back control of Arden, flooding their magic back into the forest that had once been famed as enchanted. From there the freed fairies would flood through the Gate Sinister into the mortal world again, swarming upon Britannia with a desire to avenge themselves upon the descendants of Queen Bess's pet magician.

Without the sacrifice of Gloucester blood, her mother's rage could not extend beyond the Lake of All Worlds. Could not break the banks of their prison. But that was little comfort when Flavia was about to be murdered in that same lake. She sank beneath the brackish, ill-tasting water once again. This time, she was barely able to lift her head, gasping for air.

Her mother would never forgive her. Flavia would never take up the seat in the Court of Gloriana that had been held for her (so she was promised) since she was born. She would spend the rest of her life among mortals, hiding the colour of her skin and pretending to be something she was not.

She would actually have to *be* a governess.

Hard upon that thought was the other thought, the realisation that she had come so close to giving up those children. They would have been separated from their family, trapped between Arden and Faerie forever so that their blood might keep the Gate Sinister open, that the ways between worlds would be free.

Flavia had so nearly destroyed those children. She still might. If she did not survive this, Queenie and Dash would never find their way out of their enchanted sleep to get home and safe.

Wet, springy willow branches coiled tightly around her wrists and ankles, biting deep into the flesh as Flavia fought to keep her head above the surface. "Mother, I'm sorry," she wept. Her words were empty. She regretted the consequences, but she could never regret the choice she had made. She had no strength left in her. Her broken arm burned with a fire she had never felt before.

"I made you and I can tear you back to stems and petals," the Queen roared.

"Hold there!" said a cheerful voice.

Flavia's head whipped up to see who had interrupted them. Whoops and hollers exploded all around her, along with a great deal of splashing. Two men dashed forth with shining metal in their hands, attacking the weeping willow's trailing branches.

Tanaquil Gloriana screamed in fury.

Green-black sap fountained up out of the tree trunk as one of the howling heroes hacked into it with his blade. Flavia turned her head away as the goo slopped messily over her, acrid and smelling of fish blood and treacle. The angry scream of Flavia's mother echoed inside her head, and the willow branches tightened ferociously around her broken arm.

In that instant, Flavia knew that her mother was

withdrawing to the Isle, and that she intended to take Flavia with her.

Flavia dug her heels deep in the mud, throwing herself backwards against the bank and concentrating all her magical as well as physical strength on being *free*, whatever the cost. Agony lanced through her arm, a harsh blaze of pain that whited out her vision and left her gasping.

Then it was gone. The pain, the noise, her mother, the awful thunderous pressure. The lake was silent. It was all gone.

Including, she realised a few moments later, her right arm.

~

A great deal of gumption was still required to survive this particular night's activities. Flavia was not certain she had any left. She summoned a skerrick of gumption, barely a crumb, and used her left hand to free herself, breaking the willow fronds that still wound around her legs. They fell limply into the water around her, no longer murderous nor living.

Two sap-stained young men in torn shirts helped her out of the waters of the lake, looking guilty and horrified. She could see now that they were not armed with swords or knives but with hammers, chisels and in the case of Mr Rinaldo Device, a small pickaxe. Cold iron. They had smuggled cold iron into the Forest of Arden.

Who on earth did they think they were?

"My lady, consider yourself rescued," said Orlando Device with a sweeping bow. He was trying to be polite, but his eyes kept darting to her (lack of) arm in consternation. "Are you — quite well?"

Flavia was not bleeding, and the pain had become a dull ache. What remained of her magic was staunching the wound, protecting her from the enormity of how badly she was hurt. Still. This would not do.

She stared at the two rumpled gentlemen for one long moment, and pushed herself to her feet. Then she turned and walked unsteadily back into the thicker part of the forest, soaked and stinking of dead tree, ignoring her rescuers. One foot in front of the other. Back to her children.

PALACE SCANDAL: ROYAL WEDDING SPARKS FLY!

Word among the ton is that two former darlings of Buckingham Palace, Messrs Device and Device, are no longer the favourites of HRM after an unfortunate incident at a recent royal wedding.

Why have the lovely Princess Y and her Cornish bridegroom not been seen in public since the happy day? Official word insists that they are honeymooning privately on the continent, and yet the princess's maid was spotted this week in the grounds of Buckingham Palace. That suggests her mistress, at least, has not travelled far from home.

What was so scandalous about the entertainment provided by the Extraordinary and Miraculous Device Brothers at the royal wedding? Why have they been banished from

the Court? Not one of the guests present at that
fateful wedding breakfast will spill the beans...

— A London Gossip, *The Spark and*
Philtre Gazette, 1878

Chapter 9

In Which the Highly Improbable is Discarded to Make Way for Ineffable Truths

D amp and bemused, Rinaldo watched the fairy governess stagger away from them, trailing lake water and tree sap in her wake.

"Well," said Orlando finally. "There's gratitude for you." He sniffed his muddy shirt, and pulled his shirt ends out so as to wring water out of them.

Rinaldo smacked him vaguely on the back, still in shock. "Her arm — I'm not imagining that, am I? They ripped her whole bloody arm off. Should we follow her?"

"She still seems to have both her feet," said Orlando. "She's not even bleeding, did you notice?"

"She doesn't look at all well," Rinaldo fretted. "In shock, perhaps?"

"Green about the gills."

This time Rinaldo smacked his brother over the head. "Come on. Let's see where she goes."

Miss Wednesday was not what Rinaldo had imagined a fairy would look like, based on the limited book selection available in the orphanage. She was no sylph-like waif child with gossamer wings, rosy cheeks and wide eyes. She looked like – well, a governess, more than anything. Albeit a governess whose generous (and unexpectedly grass-coloured) figure was currently wrapped in wet petticoat and lake moss.

She walked confidently, though there was something addled about her – more than once, she came close to smacking straight into a tree. Despite her erratic behaviour, she moved with purpose.

At one point she stopped, and had a noisy cry for a few moments, all shudders and choking sobs. The Brothers Device stood awkwardly nearby, pretending not to notice. Then they moved on as before – she leading, they following.

Finally, she emerged from the trees and headed down a familiar slope towards the giant topiary chessboard.

"I told you there was something odd about that place," Orlando hissed to Rinaldo.

"What the hell's she doing here?" Rinaldo whispered back.

"Same thing as us," said Orlando, at a normal volume. "She's up to no good. A conjunction of crim-

inal activity on All Hallow's Eve – Master Dickens
will probably write a novel about us."

"He might," said Rinaldo. "If he hadn't been dead
for nearly a decade."

Miss Wednesday touched the ground lightly as she
made her wavering path across the chessboard lawn in
her damp and ragged petticoats. She staggered
between a muddle of peacocks, griffins and what had to
be a sphinx with a bishop's mitre upon its head. Almost
immediately, a great burst of flame exploded from
within the cluster of hedges.

Unexpected fire was something with which both
Device brothers were greatly experienced. Hardly a
day of genius inventing went by without something
exploding into flames, deadly poisonous steam, or some
other danger. Orlando rolled, removed his flameproof
coat, and then took a running leap into the burning
topiary with the coat in his hands.

Rinaldo hesitated only a few moments before
hurtling after his brother. He rather thought it might
be better to keep his own flameproof coat on (they had
cost half a fortune apiece) but once he was in the thick
of the hedges and smoke, he realised that his brother
had made the smarter decision. Miss Wednesday was
choking and singed and now wrapped in Orlando's
coat, but there were two children too, a boy and a girl
scrying. In all the confusion, it took far too long for
Rinaldo to take his own coat off and bundle up the
children.

Still, it was accomplished with no one dead at the end, and that was better than they could have expected.

The five of them retreated to the centre of the grass chessboard, to cough and splutter and clear their lungs of the smoke.

"You were kidnapping us, weren't you, Miss Wednesday?" said the young girl in a clear voice, when they could all speak again. Her eyes were bright and angry, and her braids were coming unravelled. Rinaldo recognised her as Miss Gloucester, the daughter of the big house. The boy was Master Dashmond, who had been so fascinated by Orlando and the automaton at the fair. Was that earlier today? No explanation came forth about the cause of the flames.

Orlando opened his mouth as if he was about to say something cheerfully inappropriate. Rinaldo elbowed him firmly in the ribs, and his brother closed his mouth again.

Miss Wednesday sagged on the grass, still green from fingers to hair. "Yes," she said, sounding thoroughly fed up. "I'm afraid I was. I'm sorry, Queenie. I've made a hash of everything."

"What happened to your arm?" Dashmond blurted.

Rinaldo was glad someone had asked that question. How could a person survive such a loss?

The Gloucester girl caught hold of her brother's hand and stood over Miss Wednesday, brimming over with a childish fury worse than that of the fairies they had faced so recently. "Why? Why would you do this to us?"

"Can I be so bold as to suggest that this is not the place for extended storytelling?" Orlando broke in. "I'm concerned about a number of hedge monsters that might be roaming the area. One of them pursued us not so long ago."

The girl turned her sharp gaze upon him instead. "You were those charlatans at the village fair. Why are you here?"

"They're not charlatans, they made a mechanical man out of spoons!" Master Dashmond protested. He was enjoying this adventure rather more than his sister.

"Orlando is right," admitted Rinaldo. "The time for discussion is when we are out of Arden and back in the world of mortals."

Miss Gloucester looked around, as if realising for her first time where they were. "This can't be the Forest of *Arden*. That's nonsense. It's a fairy tale."

"You don't even read fairy tales," her brother said. "What would you know?"

Orlando reclaimed his coat from Miss Wednesday, shook it out with a flourish and then put it back on himself. "Just because something is a fairy tale does not mean we're not standing in it."

~

The arm was going to be a problem. There would be questions about it — questions enough about this night's work. It was more than an inconvenience. But Flavia could not risk using more magic, not this close to Faerie.

She allowed the Device brothers to take charge, leading them all back along the chamomile path and towards the Gate Sinister. Walking silently along with the rest of the party, Flavia began to recover her usual composure.

I can do this.

Queenie marched at a great pace as if to remind everyone that she had not forgotten their promise of explanations at the end of their escape. Dash, cheerful but exhausted, took turns to be carried by the Device brothers, who swung him up on their shoulders and backs with goodnatured cheer.

It was almost companionable, though Flavia could still feel Queenie's accusing gaze darting back at her. She did not blame her. How could the children trust her now?

"There it is," called Mr Rinaldo Device, up ahead of them. "The gateway."

Flavia looked up and saw the ornamental stones and trellis of the Gate Sinister and beyond it, the moonlit garden of Gloucester Worth. She quickened her step, hurrying out of the Forest of Arden.

The night air was cold around her and the air

suddenly tasted of the end of autumn instead of a stale spring. Flavia's legs were unsteady, and her missing arm ached. It had been severed a little above the elbow, but she could still feel the length of it, the soreness all the way down to fingers that no longer existed. (She could still feel the snap from where Quicksilver broke her bone between her deft hands.)

Flavia sank down on to the grass in the grounds of Gloucester Worth. She had never been so glad to feel the disapproving presence of the house nearby. The others fell around her like playing cards, settling on the ground. When she looked up, Flavia saw that the Gate Sinister had returned to being a simple garden arch again, not a way to another world. All Hallows had ended.

They sat in silence for a short while upon the damp grass, recovering from their adventure.

"Now," said Queenie, lifting her chin. "I want answers."

Flavia swallowed.

"We'll start, if we may," said Mr Orlando Device, with a gallant nod of his head. He was the most rumpled of all of them, except perhaps Flavia in the still-drying petticoats that made her completely indecent for mixed company.

Orlando Device looked somewhat indecent himself, his shirt ripped and charred and hanging half-open beneath his coat. Flavia blinked, and then looked at him covertly beneath her eyelashes. He really was horrendously pretty, for a human. It was unsettling. If he was female, she might be in danger of swooning in his presence.

"Will we, indeed?" said Rinaldo with a sharp look in his brother's direction. Flavia looked away, not wanting to be caught staring at either of them.

"It's the gentlemanly thing to do," said Orlando.

"Indeed," said Queenie, acting every inch like her mother, all haughty and cold. "Tell us what you were doing in the Forest of Arden, if there really *is* such a place. And then our *trusted* governess can tell us why Dashmond and I were taken there without our consent."

"Of course there's such a place," said Dash. "Don't you read anything, Queenie? Arden is where all the stories of fairy knights and enchantresses and magic fountains come from."

"Magic fountains," Queenie said scornfully. "Rot and bunkum."

Orlando patted Dash on the shoulder. "The lad has the right of it, Miss Queenie. That is why my brother and myself were there tonight, to collect the enchanted waters on behalf of our employer. We were told that for one night only, this All Hallows, the gateway would be open." His eyes darted in Flavia's direction.

"I opened it," said Flavia curtly. "The Gate Sinister is old magic, blood magic. Who told you it would be open?" She had informed no one of her quest; had no friends in this entire world to share her secrets with. Only the Queen and her court had known she would be here.

Rinaldo Device met her gaze with his own, dark and thoughtful. She found his presence oddly comforting. He seemed so much steadier than his brother. "A wicked enchantress sent us," he said. "She knows many things. She must have known you would be here too."

"What enchantress?" Flavia asked.

The only way that a mortal enchantress could have known that Queenie and Dashmond would open the Gate Sinister on this particular night was if she had learned it from the Queen of Faerie. Her mother had set up some other scheme this night, beyond Flavia's quest. Had Flavia always been expendable?

"Her name is Lady Elspeth Mortmain," said Orlando. "I believe she is related to the Gloucester family by marriage..."

"She's our aunt," said Dash as if this was an obvious thing that they all should have known. "Is Aunt Elspeth a wicked enchantress? No wonder Mother is always so funny about her."

"My brother and I fell on hard times recently," Orlando continued. "Lady Mortmain took advantage of our need. She is holding certain artefacts of ours hostage against our goodwill and sent us on a quest to earn them back."

"Surprisingly tactful summary," agreed Rinaldo.

"What was your quest?" Flavia asked, using her stern governess voice to full effect.

Orlando spread his hands wide in a dramatic fashion. "A trivial matter, accomplished with flair."

Lying, or misdirecting. Flavia stared flatly at him, and Orlando broke easily enough. That was another trick she had picked up from the mistresses at the School of Good Wives and God's Mercy. Silence and a hard stare could be an effective weapon.

"Draughts from the magical fountains," Orlando confessed. "Worth a great deal to a person of the magical persuasion. Nothing like a fresh supply of Love-Me-Not to get yourself through the London season without contracting a foolish marriage."

Curious. He was still lying, or at least not telling all of the truth. But this time, he had landed upon an effective misdirection.

"Love-Me-Not?" Queenie repeated incredulously. "Are you saying — what are you saying?" The girl vibrated with even more anger than before. "You expect me to believe that Aunt Elspeth is an enchantress, and that Love-Me-Not comes from a *fountain*?"

The Device brothers glanced at each other, and then at the furious girl. "But of course," said Orlando. "I didn't realise that would be the hard part to swallow."

"Love-Me-Not is a highly valuable lost formula," Queenie argued. "My great-grandfather's fortune was founded upon the brewing of that philtre. I've been working for years to replicate his work. You can't dredge it out of a *fountain*."

Orlando seemed unbothered by her fury. "Love-Me-Not is rare because it's the most coveted and prized philtre of Britannian history, and there was only ever one supply line. It dried up when Richard Gloucester — the first Earl of Shuttlesworth — died, and his secret was thought to have died with him. Magic practitioners in high circles have always known where it came from, just not how to get there. I suppose Lady Mortmain worked out that your family's blood was the key to the gate."

Queenie leapt to her feet. "The Love-Me-Not is right there, in that forest? I can — send a bucket down a well to collect it? I have Gloucester blood! I can do it right now."

Flavia caught at the girl's skirt with her remaining hand. "Queenie, no."

"Don't you dare," Queenie hurled at her. "Don't you dare try to stop me, *Miss Wednesday,* if that is even your real name. This is the answer to all my hopes, and you knew it all along! My inheritance!"

"I know that you can't reopen the gate now," Flavia said sharply, using her most authoritative voice, though her throat was still sore from all the screaming she had done by the lakeside. "It's nearly morning. Look to the dawn."

Queenie tugged her skirts angrily away from

Flavia's hands and turned back to Orlando. She held her hand out imperiously. "Give me the draught you collected for Lady Mortmain so that I can test it. Aunt Elspeth has no business sticking her nose into our family fountains. She's Mama's sister, barely related to the Gloucesters at all. She may be allowed to live in our town house, but she's not going to get her hands on my great-grandfather's philtre!"

Orlando Device was amused. "You'll have to be more convincing than that, Miss Queenie. Your aunt is far more terrifying than you. Besides, I took a sample from every fountain tonight, and they're unmarked. The only way to be sure which philtre is which is to drink a drop. Do you volunteer?"

"It might be the only way for *you*," Queenie said scornfully. "But I know something about alchemy, and the testing of philtres." She sat back on the grass with her arms crossed, not willing to let this go.

"It is indeed nearly morning," said Rinaldo, looking at the light as it edged up over the garden around them. "We should be away to London."

"Not just yet, Professor," said Orlando, and gave Flavia a smile far less charming than what he usually had to offer. "We're not the only one with secrets to spill. Don't you think, Miss Wednesday? I'm agog to hear your version of tonight's events."

She owed them nothing. They had saved her, yes, they had been *useful*, but that didn't mean they had earned her secrets. She was certain that Orlando Device had left much out of his own tale.

But Flavia had to tell the children the truth, and it would be easier to do this in front of witnesses.

"You don't have to," Rinaldo said quickly. "Not if it pains you." There was a kindness in his eyes, a sympathy that made her want to cry.

"Everything pains me," Flavia confessed in a low voice. Dash was half-asleep, and might not remember anything she said, but Queenie was wide awake and deserved her explanation.

"Let's start with an easy one," said Orlando, his eyes bright with anticipation. "Are you a fairy, Miss Wednesday?"

Flavia breathed out, and something flew free inside her. "Yes," she said. "I am a fairy. I was sent into the mortal world on a dandelion seed, to free the fairies from their exile."

And I failed.

After two years of deep mourning for her late husband, the widowed Queen Isolda returned to public life in 1867 with renewed vigour. She had at this time been the ruling monarch of Britannia for more than two decades, but it was this period as 'the iron widow' that cemented her reputation as a canny political leader and a dominant force of nature.

Over the following decade, the Iron Widow acquired new titles at a startling rate, culminating in the declaration that with the annexation of India, Britannia was now the crown of an Empire. As the Empress of Britannia, India and beyond, Queen Isolda championed science over magic at every turn, funding various institutions and scholarships. She also took an interest in anti-fairy propaganda, commissioning plays and novels that emphasised the role her distant ancestor, Queen Elizabeth Tudor, had in the banishing of fairy magic from Britannia.

During this period, the reputation of Queen Elizabeth, a formerly despised monarch, was reframed in Britannian folklore as 'Good Queen Bess,' the enemy of wild magic and patron of modern arts and sciences. Queen Isolda clothed herself and her daughters in fashions of the Elizabethan era, to ensure all Britannians associated her with the deeds of that beloved former queen. She sponsored practitioners of magic whose approach to the art was more mechanical than miraculous. Her rising power and public image relied heavily on an implicit promise that the fairies would never return to her lands.

— "How Queen Isolda Fought the First Fairy Renaissance," Dahlia Peasebottom, *The Journal of Botanical Sorcery Vol 18* (1972)

Chapter 10

Of Philtres and Fairies

Flavia reached out with her left hand, plucking closed-up daisies and clover from the shadowy lawn around them, making a little heap of them in her lap. "Many centuries ago, Good Queen Bess fought a duel with my true mother, Tanaquil Gloriana, Queen of the Faerie." Flavia waited for the hiss and whisper of grasses and tree branches in response to her mother's name, but there was nothing but silence. Her breath stuck in her throat for a moment.

"Easy does it," Orlando urged. "Guilty secrets are best shared in the right order, so as not to unsettle the stomach."

"Gloriana lost," said Flavia, her fingers twirling absently at the flowers in her lap. "She and the kingdom of Faerie were banished for three generations to their Isle, in the Lake of All Worlds in the Forest of

Arden. She and her people accepted that ruling grudgingly, but then Queen Bess broke the accord. She had her magicians closet the Forest of Arden away from the world of mortals by building the Gate Sinister, so that my mother's people would be trapped forever. One of those magicians was an ancestor of the Gloucester family."

She looked up. Both Device gentlemen wore grave faces. Queenie's eyes were cast down as if she could not bear to look at Flavia. Dash leaned against Rinaldo, still wrapped in the gentleman's too-big coat. The boy's eyes were bright pinpricks of tiredness.

"Centuries passed," Flavia went on, the fingers of her left hand busily knotting the daisies together with grass and clover and a twig or two of the nearest hawthorn bush, no longer bright with mayblossom. "Gloriana's people remained trapped. They called to the world of mortals, year after year, hoping that someone would find their way into the forest and free them. All they needed was a hairline crack in those magics, to free themselves. And he came eventually, a man descended from one of the original magicians. He discovered a sliver of light in his garden, where there had once been a pathway into Arden. He opened the Gate Sinister using blood magic, and ensured that only he and his own blood relatives could open it again in the future."

"My great-grandfather," said Queenie, eyes bright at this revelation.

"Richard Gloucester." Flavia agreed. "A young man, then, of moderate wealth and minor nobility, but not for long. Over the years, he stripped Arden of its magical philtres, siphoning them from the fountains to build his fortune. But he kept his distance from the Lake of All Worlds. He resisted the call of Faerie, resisted every blandishment or temptation for decades. He married, had children, furnished his house richly, and sold philtres to the aristocracy. It was a wild time in London, with magic and potions the very height of fashion. Antidotes were worth more than their weight in gold, and thanks to his visits to the forest, Richard Gloucester had the one antidote that no one else could supply: Love-Me-Not."

Queenie made a small humphing noise, but Flavia ignored her and went on. "He was credited with saving Queen Isolda's grandfather, George IV, from several unfortunate attempts to trap him into marriage, after the death of Queen Caroline. He named Richard Gloucester an Earl."

"He tricked them all," Queenie said sullenly. "He made the world think he was a great scientist for inventing that philtre, when he *cheated* by taking it from a fairy fountain."

"He supplied a great and useful service," Orlando corrected. "Where would we be today without Love-Me-Not?"

"Where would you be, you mean?" Rinaldo

muttered. "And there isn't much of it around, these days, in case you've forgotten."

"That may change now that we've located the original supply," said Orlando with a wicked grin, patting his pockets.

Queenie looked like she wanted to throttle Orlando with her bare hands, and rob him of his bounty.

"Richard Gloucester grew old, and was widowed," Flavia went on. The muddle of clover and daisies and hawthorn in her lap grew larger. She wove threads of grass in and out of the pattern with her single hand. "The fairies feared that he was their last chance of escape, so they took desperate measures. Gloriana sacrificed dozens of her loyal knights to raise the power necessary to swim the breadth of the Lake of All Worlds, hoping she could seduce him into claiming her as his wife from the shore. A marital bond might be enough to break the original spells – especially as it would tie her and any child she had by blood to the Gloucesters. Again, he refused her."

She looked across and saw that Dash had finally fallen asleep. "Richard Gloucester made one last visit to the Forest of Arden before he died, drawing a final cask of Love-Me-Not from the fountain. He bid farewell to the fairies across the lake. And when he came home – they sent something after him, something so tiny that he did not even notice they had done it. A dandelion seed, floating on the wind, clinging to the back of his coat."

Neither of the Device brothers looked remotely surprised by this revelation.

"You," whispered Queenie, her eyes wide and her hands trembling.

"I remembered none of it, growing up," Flavia admitted. "Not until I fell into Faerie through my dreams, and they told me I had been sent to the mortal world on a vital mission, to release them all from their exile." It was a strange kind of relief to be spilling the story out after keeping it hidden for so long.

"That was tonight," said Queenie, the brains of her family after all. "You were supposed to release them tonight."

"Yes," said Flavia. "The Gate Sinister was bonded to the blood of Richard Gloucester's line. But so were the spells of exile, long ago, because of his ancestor's role in the banishment. My mother planned to use your mortal blood to break our people free, and restore the Forest of Arden. Once the fairies had the Gate, they could open all the old ways up again, the many paths to and from Arden across Britannia. Fairies would return to the world of mortals, to come and go as they pleased."

"That's what we need, another war with Faerie," Rinaldo muttered to Orlando. "The last one went so well."

"You read too much history," snorted his brother.

"You intended to give us to her," said Queenie, moving a little closer to her sleeping brother. "You came to this house to *kidnap* us."

"Yes," said Flavia, refusing to apologise for it again. "I stole you, and then I changed my mind, and I betrayed my own people. And now, I don't know what to do."

There was a long silence.

"Was he your father?" Orlando asked, breaking that silence with an impressive display of tactlessness. Rinaldo elbowed him, hard, but it was too late. "Richard Gloucester."

"I've always thought so," Flavia admitted, embarrassed by this final revelation. "Symbolically if not... well, you can never quite tell, with fairies."

Queenie gave her a very hard stare. "But that means — are you my *Aunt?*"

"Great-aunt, surely," Orlando teased.

"Keep out of it," Rinaldo told him with an exasperated look.

"It doesn't matter," Flavia said. "I am a fairy, and if I have any of Richard Gloucester's blood in me, it is not pure enough to affect the Gate Sinister. Not human enough. Believe me, my mother would have broken free years ago if all it took was sacrificing *me*. I was a failed experiment."

"Of course it doesn't matter," said Queenie, remaining horribly calm. "Bastard children don't count in the line of succession."

Flavia felt as if she had been slapped, which undoubtedly was Queenie's intention.

"Family isn't always about blood," said Rinaldo, speaking up unexpectedly. "Sometimes it's about who you choose to stick around for. Who chooses you."

"Soppy bugger," said Orlando, punching him on the arm.

"Shut up, I was making a point."

"I have no claim on the Gloucester family, nor do I expect them to claim me," said Flavia stiffly. She had never had anyone she could count on, wouldn't fool herself into thinking she could have that from Queenie and Dash, not now.

She still would protect them, and she didn't have to be an aunt to do that.

"When can Dash and I return to the forest?" Queenie asked in a businesslike tone of voice. "Tomorrow night?"

"Never," said Orlando and Rinaldo in unison.

Flavia should lie to Queenie. Arden was not a safe place for children, even children whose blood granted them access. No wonder the adult Gloucesters were so worried about their children's magical abilities, with a threat like this lurking in their garden.

But she was tired of dissembling. Fairies hid their faces, never their thoughts and words. At least, that was what she had always been taught.

She had no mask to hide behind. Time for the truth.

"You must never come back here without a strong and capable *adult* practitioner of magic," Flavia told Queenie. "There are perils in the Forest of Arden — my mother most perilous of all if you stray too near the lake. But at certain times of the year, yes, it might be possible."

Dash was fast asleep at Rinaldo's feet. He at least would not discover this tantalising truth, unless Queenie was irresponsible enough to share it with him.

"Certain days," said Queenie, frowning. "Like the Hallows, spring and autumn? And the Solstices?"

Flavia did her best to hide her surprise. "Indeed."

"That part wasn't hard to guess," the girl frowned. "Great-Grandfather only ever produced new batches of his philtre the day after a Hallows or a Solstice. It says so in his journals. I thought it was a clue as to one of the ingredients, perhaps a time when they had to be picked." There was a hint of melancholy in her voice. The great mystery of her family had been solved, and not in a way that she liked.

Queenie turned her head towards the garden arch, which now led through to an antique rose walk with marble statues of the Muses. "You'd better stay on as our governess," she said finally. "You will, won't you?"

Flavia was more than surprised. "You want me to stay? After what I did to you and Dash?"

"Exactly," said Queenie. There was no warmth in her voice. "You owe us. You work for me, now. If there is a way to restore my family fortune and save me from a love philtre marriage, you will make it happen."

Blackmail, then. "What if I choose to leave?" Not that Flavia had anywhere else to go.

"Then you won't be here to stop me going alone at the Winter Solstice," said Queenie with satisfaction. "I *will* find the Love-Me-Not and restore my family's fortune, with or without your help. If you don't want me wandering around in the Forest of Arden unprotected, you'd better stay by my side."

Flavia considered what little she had in the way of choice. This way, she could keep her place at Gloucester Worth, which would buy her time to decide what to do with a future she never imagined.

Was she prepared to be a mortal governess forever, at the mercy of this little tyrant and her brother?

Instead of answering the girl right away, Flavia concentrated on her missing arm. Here in the garden, this was her last chance to reach out and use some magic before the oppressive weight of Gloucester Worth swallowed her up again.

Flavia lifted the messy net of flower scraps and grass that she had been weaving together. She whispered a dream song to it, breathing in magic from the plants and trees around her. The net twisted and grew, extending tendrils like tree roots that caught upon the stump of her missing right arm.

They watched her, all of them, staring shamelessly. She blocked them out as she built herself a replacement limb, one clover leaf at a time, bending and shaping the magic until she had the silhouette of fingers, of a wrist that matched her other.

It was green, of course. She could cast an illusion on it when she needed to conceal the colour, but the shape of the flowers and leaves would still show through. There was a limit to how much magic you could pile on top of other magic. Gloves, at least, were expected for a young lady of her station to wear under most circumstances.

"The fingers are too long," said Rinaldo in a choked-off voice.

Flavia took the criticism as constructive, lined the new arm up against the one made of flesh, and shortened the fingers, so that they matched.

"You use plants like I use metal," he said abruptly.

Flavia glanced up, meeting his eyes with a wry smile. "I never have before," she said.

"You mean – you learned how to do that from watching me?"

She flexed her new fingers, testing their reach. "I found your technique inspiring."

Rinaldo's face was full of surprise and warmth. "How would you have done it if you hadn't seen my technique?"

"A tree branch," Flavia said carelessly, bending her new elbow. "But it wouldn't have the same range of articulation."

Rinaldo huffed a laugh at that. "Glad to be of

service, Miss Wednesday." As if realising he had been staring too long, he shook Dash half awake and hauled him to his feet, passing the boy over to Flavia.

Queenie brushed grass off her own skirt in a businesslike fashion. She regarded the Device brothers critically. "You're both rather handy," she said. "If you stay around to help with my endeavours, I can make it worth your while financially."

Clearly, she still had not given up hope of relieving Orlando of his pockets full of philtres.

Orlando disguised a laugh with a cough. "Generous offer, miss," he said. "But we'll be off to London, to get our own lives out of hock. If all goes well, we'll be sitting pretty, and if we fail, we need to put as much distance between ourselves and Isolda's Britannia as possible."

"The South of France is a fine place to wait out the winter," said Rinaldo, sounding hopeful. "Spain, perhaps?"

"Egypt," said Orlando with a dazzling grin aimed at his brother. "I've always wanted to see the pyramids. And don't tell me you haven't thought about Bombay."

Flavia shook both of their hands politely. They were amiable enough company, but it would put her mind at ease to know that the witnesses of tonight's events were a goodly distance from herself and the two Gloucester children.

"Thank you," she said. "For everything."

Orlando's hand lingered on hers longer than she

expected, and then he took the other – the one she had made from daisies and clover – and kissed it lightly. Rinaldo elbowed his brother, and offered Flavia an apologetic grin.

"It gets better with practice," he said in an undertone. "The family thing. Even if you've never done it before."

"These children are not my family," Flavia said firmly, but Rinaldo shrugged and doffed an imaginary top hat to her.

"Let it be a work in progress," were his parting words.

Flavia, Queenie and a half-asleep Dash stood and watched as the Miraculous and Extraordinary Device Brothers sauntered out of the garden.

"That's them out of the way," said the girl. Her voice was sharp and unrelenting. "And so? Will you be our governess, for the foreseeable future?"

"Oh yes," said Flavia Wednesday, gazing at the arm she had built out of clover, and then up at the house that had hated her since she first crossed its threshold. "I'll be your governess. I'll keep you safe."

The grass whispered at them, as Flavia escorted the two tired children inside, but she would not listen to anything it had to say.

She had a new mission now.

END

Afterword

Thank you so much for reading the first novella in the Sparks & Philtres series! Flavia, the Gloucester family and the Extraordinary and Miraculous Device Brothers will return in...

HOUSE PERILOUS
(SPARKS & PHILTRES #2)

A Tale of Vengeful Fairies, Governessing in Town Houses, The Great Exhibition, Potion-Induced Amnesia, A False Fountain, Magical Artifice & the Science of Miracles in 19th Century Britannia.

Meanwhile, I would be delighted if you chose to review this book at your book vendor of choice.

About the Author

Tansy Rayner Roberts is an award-winning Australian science fiction and fantasy author who enjoys quilting and obscure historiography. She lives with her family in Tasmania and has the complete opposite of botanical magic.

- Listen to Tansy on *Sheep Might Fly*, a podcast where she reads aloud her stories as audio serials.
- Read Tansy's stories before anyone else when you pledge to her Patreon: patreon.com/tansyrr
- What tea is Tansy drinking? Find out when you subscribe to her excellent newsletter.
- Follow Tansy at Bookbub so you never miss a release.

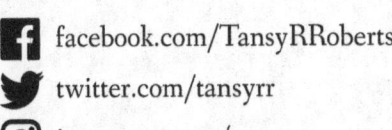 facebook.com/TansyRRoberts

twitter.com/tansyrr

instagram.com/tansyrr

Also by Tansy Rayner Roberts

Tea & Sympathetic Magic

There's nothing more dangerous than an eligible duke...

Every eligible young lady of the Teacup Isles wants to marry the Duke of Storm, except Miss Mnemosyne Seabourne, who is quite content on the shelf, thank you very much. All she wants is a quiet life and a good book.

At a house party full of ruthless debutantes willing to employ sneaky sympathetic magic to win a husband of quality, Mneme joins forces with an enigmatic spellcracker to rescue the duke from being married against his will.

Can Mneme save the Duke of Storm without becoming his bride? Will this caper ruin her reputation forever? Can teacups and hedgehogs be used as projectile weapons in emergencies? Why are attractive men more devastating when they roll up their sleeves?

If you enjoy Regency house parties, witty romantic banter and high society sorcery, you'll adore this magical comedy of manners cosy mystery novella.

The Frost Fair Affair

Our heroine stumbles across a precarious plot while printing political pamphlets...

Thanks to last Season's scandal involving her family, Miss Mnemosyne Seabourne is officially notorious. Wintering in Town, she hopes to use her new celebrity to campaign about the unfair restriction on portal travel for ladies... while being quietly courted by a certain handsome spellcracker.

As the river freezes over and a spectacular Frost Fair sets up on the ice, Mneme finds herself beset by secret societies, spies and sneaky saboteurs. Who stole her political pamphlets? Who is leaving dead bodies around printing presses for anyone to find?

Mr Thornbury knows more than he's letting on. If she can't trust the man she hoped to marry, Mneme is just going to have to unravel the mystery for herself, quick enough to save both of their lives.

If you enjoy vintage spy adventures, flirtatious couples and cosy sleigh rides, you'll adore this exciting sequel to *Tea and Sympathetic Magic*.

Spellcracker's Honeymoon

Our honeymooning heroine must unmask a magical murderer.

Happily married, Mrs Mnemosyne Seabourne travels to an island of no magic, for a relaxing honeymoon with her new husband, Thornbury.

But the magic-free Isle of Aster is not what it seems. There's a monster roaming the hills, a royal scandal brewing on the horizon, and (of course!) an impossible, magical murder to be solved.

On the night of the Midsummer Masque at the Queen's country palace, Thornbury goes missing, leaving Mneme to unravel a web of secrets and lies involving her own husband.

Who could commit magical murder on an island with no magic? Only a spellcracker...

If you enjoy cozy magical mysteries, glamorous masquerade balls and the art of saucy letter writing, you'll love the third Teacup Magic novella.

Castle Charming

In this fairy tale kingdom, the royals of Castle Charming have always been cursed.

What will it take to heal their family, and survive the magical threat overwhelming their land?

Castle Charming is an enormously fun collection of LGBTQ+ fairy tale novellas, including:

- The cruel truth behind fairy godmothers.
- Disaster princes cursed to dance all night.
- A spinning wheel with a taste for royal blood.
- A giant attack beanstalk.
- A powerful magical princess who could destroy them all.